2

Shiloh Walker

Mythe: Vampire

D1571152

Ellora's Cave
Romantica Publishing

An Ellora's Cave Romantica Publication

www.ellorascave.com

Mythe: Vampire

ISBN # 1419952412
ALL RIGHTS RESERVED.
Mythe Vampire Copyright© 2004 Shiloh Walker
Edited by: Pamela Campbell
Cover art by: Syneca

Electronic book Publication: October, 2004
Trade paperback Publication: October, 2005

Excerpt from *Coming in Last* Copyright © Shiloh Walker, 2004

Warning:

The following material contains graphic sexual content meant for mature readers. *Mythe Vampire* has been rated *E-rotic* by a minimum of three independent reviewers.

Ellora's Cave Publishing offers three levels of Romantica™ reading entertainment: S (S-ensuous), E (E-rotic), and X (X-treme).

S-*ensuous* love scenes are explicit and leave nothing to the imagination.

E-*rotic* love scenes are explicit, leave nothing to the imagination, and are high in volume per the overall word count. In addition, some E-rated titles might contain fantasy material that some readers find objectionable, such as bondage, submission, same sex encounters, forced seductions, etc. E-rated titles are the most graphic titles we carry; it is common, for instance, for an author to use words such as "fucking", "cock", "pussy", etc., within their work of literature.

X-*treme* titles differ from E-rated titles only in plot premise and storyline execution. Unlike E-rated titles, stories designated with the letter X tend to contain controversial subject matter not for the faint of heart.

Also by Shiloh Walker:

Vampire
Mythe

Chapter One

Her hair was tangled around her face when she stepped out of the lodge. Ronal studied the mortal's slender, lithe form with the appreciation any man would have for a half-naked woman, especially one who had obviously spent most of her night engaged in some very strenuous, very physical activity.

The scent of sex and a satyr's musk drifted to him on the air and explained the wide, pleased smile that was on Arys' face as he followed her out of the cabin, brushing one hand down her hair, lowering his head to brush his lips over her cheek.

She in turn reached up and rested her hand on the satyr's cheek in a tender, sweet moment.

The vampire smiled, a slow curl of his lips, as satisfaction blazed through him. Damnation, but it was good to see the satyr smile again. It had been ages since he had been truly happy.

"Stop eying her like you plan on having her for a midday snack," Daklin drawled, his voice dry. "She's in love with Arys. Leave her alone."

Ronal raised his eyes heavenward for a brief moment before turning his gaze to a man who had aspired to be the biggest pain in his backside in half a millennium. "I have no designs on the woman. I do not even know her name, but I can see clearly enough. Her heart and her soul already belong to the satyr."

He couldn't quite smash the niggling jealousy, though. It ate at him as he rose to his feet to meet the lady when Arys led her over.

She cast her eyes to the sky, and then again at his face, squinting. "I didn't think vampires could take the sunlight," she said without preamble after Arys introduced them.

He had traveled through the night coming here, and could travel three more days without rest, without pause. As he absorbed her words and made sure he understood her, he started to chuckle. "The legends your people have of my kind are not terribly accurate," he said with a grin. "Only in part. And sunlight is not harmful to a vampire after their first century. I've enough age in me to withstand a thousand years of sunlight without any ill befalling me."

She brushed a hand over her throat, unconsciously, as his fangs flashed at her. Softly, she asked, "Ahh…what is accurate, and what is not?"

With a gentle smile, he promised, "Your blood is quite safe from me, my lady. Although if you decide the satyr is not treating you as he should, I'd be happy to be your companion for as long as you want me." He softened it with a teasing smile as he jabbed Arys in the arm before he stepped around them.

She laughed, turning to throw her arms around Arys. "Oh, he doesn't treat me at all like he should," she said, pressing a hard, quick kiss to Arys' mouth. "He treats me far better."

* * * * *

Ronal kept to the wood for the trip. Although they had left Satyr's Wood behind days ago, trees were still thick along the land they traveled and he preferred to move through them.

Though sunlight was no danger to him, it was a discomfort, too bright for his sensitive eyes.

The silence of the wood afforded him much time to think, to worry, and seethe.

Whoever was doing this would die. Slowly. Painfully.

His offspring, the breed vamp…she was dead.

He felt her loss within him when he searched for her, and she wasn't there.

He hadn't been close to Caria, his offspring's mother, in years, but his heart ached for the mother and the father. The mortal man seemed to age a decade right in front of Ronal as he softly explained to Caria and the child's birth father that he couldn't find any link to the missing breed vamp.

If she were alive, he would have been able to touch her, since he had sired her mother, brought her into the Blood to save her from dying years before. Caria had been working in a tavern and walking to her tiny lodging outside of town when three men had grabbed her.

They had raped her, and before they left, one had slit her throat, leaving her to die.

Ronal had come upon her only moments before she would have slipped beyond his reach.

A touch on her mind let him merge with her, and she had been frantic to live, in whatever capacity she could.

Bringing her over had saved her life.

And then he had ended the lives of those who had tried to kill her.

That had been two centuries ago, and it had taken her all this time to find a mortal lover, a man whose touch she didn't fear instinctively. True happiness…and now this.

After a lifetime of pain, Caria had found happiness with her mortal mate, borne a sweet babe—only to have that child murdered by an unknown enemy.

"Not unknown for long, Caria, I swear it," he murmured, touching her grieving mind with his.

He could feel her still in whatever she had been doing, and the warm stroke of her spirit against his. *I know that, Sire. It will not bring my baby back…but it helps knowing that no other need suffer her fate.*

It was little enough that he could do.

Of course, having to go into the lands of the elvish kin, that would not be a pleasure walk, he knew. True torture, dealing with the long-eared, arrogant bastards who hated his kind.

Oh, yes. This would be pleasant. All those winsome, lovely elvish ladies, and most of them so unbelievably arrogant, talking to them was an exercise in patience, having to bite his tongue more often than not. Keeping silent, when all he wanted to do was laugh at them for their arrogance.

So certain in themselves and their magick, the elves were.

Pity they weren't as invincible as they thought.

Through the trees ahead, he could see Daklin moving. Looking for the paths to his realm. The paths were magick-marked and moved of their own accord every few days. Only an elf could possibly find the magickal, unmarked paths. Another example of the elves' foolishness. They thought that alone kept them safe.

But you didn't need a path. Flood the Glynmare Forest with enough of the enemy, and they would eventually find the realm. All that was required was a leader who didn't care how many soldiers it took.

Daklin's whisper came floating through the air as he halted nearly a quarter of a mile in front of Ronal. "I've found the path...keep coming and I'll bring the others."

There was nothing to signify any path, other than the game trails here and there. Ronal moved along them as Daklin left the shelter of the trees for the wide, cobbled path several hundred feet outside the trees. Ronal watched, the memory of the black lightning blooming in his mind.

If their enemy saw them now...killing them would be so easy. Cray had taken to the skies for a while, but had returned to walk alongside Pepper and Arys, actually smiling from time to time.

All of them together.

Did their enemy know they weren't dead?

He obviously wasn't well versed with vampires, otherwise he would have known his strike was likely to fail. And there was no sense in that. Were they safe?

No...their enemy knew they were alive, at least some of them. He knew.

But the likelihood of him knowing they were together, and traveling for one of the few sanctuaries in the world, was slim. They had some time.

As Daklin led them through the wood, to the path, Ronal leaned idly against a tree. He had studied the area, and was fairly certain he had discovered the line the path followed.

Skimming his gaze upward, he studied the blue sky dappled through the trees.

Humans, vampires, dryads, so many of the people of Mythe all shared many very human qualities. They had become so civilized…and they never looked up.

If Ronal hadn't been watching the sky, he never would have seen her soaring through the treetops, leaping from branch to branch, swinging along vines, before disappearing into the thick foliage of a massive thisa oak.

What the hell…

His fangs dropped and he tensed, going on alert, but before he could even form the words to warn the other Pillars, the bushes at his side parted and a long, slim creature dashed out, knocking Daklin off his feet…

Daklin swore and flipped her as Ronal flew to his side, but then he stopped, cocking his head.

They were laughing, their golden locks flowing together and mingling until you couldn't see where Daklin's hair ended and the woman's started.

As Daklin lifted up, his elbows planted on the earth beside the elvish woman's head, Ronal felt everything inside him freeze.

Bloody hell, even for an elvish lady, she was…breathtaking.

"My cousin, Caetria…"

Ronal shook his head, tearing his eyes away from her face as Daklin assisted her to her feet, gently brushing leaves and twigs from her hair. "Your cousin?" Ronal repeated.

He felt her eyes on him, assessing, appraising, full of female interest. She smiled at him, but he didn't smile back.

Cousin.

Hell.

But the smile faded from her face as Daklin introduced him. "Ronal de Amshe, Lord of North Cel, my friend —"

"Friend?" she repeated coolly, in flawless Mitaro.

Daklin rested a hand on her shoulder. "Aye, friend."

"The sky must be falling," she said coldly, jerking away. "The day the elves befriend vampire scum is the day the world will end."

She was gone before Daklin's blush had finished forming.

"Well, that went rather well," the elf muttered as irritation and embarrassment heated his cheeks. The elves were known for their hospitality...hot or cold, you didn't forget the welcoming they gave you. If it had been anybody but one of the Pillars she had insulted, Daklin could have overlooked it.

As it was, Ronal couldn't help but grin at the chagrin in the elf's eyes. "Indeed. She didn't go for her knife as she so obviously wished to," he replied. "Do not dwell on it. We knew I wouldn't be welcome here. Let's go. We have no time to waste."

* * * * *

Caetria held to the trees as the small band passed by, hundreds of feet beneath her. What the bloody hell was the world coming to? More and more children being brought in from the Gates, and after they had been cared for, it was time to foster some of them out to the world beyond their realm. So more and more elves left the realm, some never coming back.

Her father was pushing her to wed, subtly, as only he could. But the pressure was still there.

Her mount had gone mad and the unicorn had to be sent on to the next world, something she still hadn't forgiven herself for. What had taken the beast so?

And now they had a vampire in their wood.

With an elf walking at his side. Not just any elf either, but a Gatekeeper, her cousin, and one of the princes of the Realm.

Daklin had gone mad. That was the explanation. Whatever had infected Ipetria had also taken her cousin's mind and he was no longer capable of good judgment.

Oh, she damn well knew the vampire was a Gatekeeper, and he may well be a good one. But that didn't make him fit company for her people. By the Father, his kind had damn near annihilated hers several millennia ago. It did not matter that the historians of Mythe claimed the elves had started the war. It mattered that they had damn near been wiped out by it.

Vampires...not fit for anything more than scavenging, and they were made Lords now. Made Gatekeepers, feared and respected.

But not *here*. They would gain no respect in her land.

Not while she was the princess, not while her father ruled the Realm.

* * * * *

14

Ronal kept his hands linked loosely behind him as Daklin introduced him to the *Esri*, the Elvish King of the Realm. Matiro was a solemn-eyed, grim-faced elf with yards of silvery brown locks that he kept woven back from his sharp-featured face in a series of tight, intricate braids.

Like Daklin, he wore a piercing in his right ear, but instead of gold, the hoop was fashioned of *diame*, a silvery metal the elves mined in the mountains to the east. Stronger than diamonds, and just as lovely, it was a prized element, wanted and sought after by many.

And the elves didn't share.

Only kings and high lords could afford the few inferior supplies of *diame* that elves allowed out of their realm.

A simple coronet, set with a blue tiger's-eye, was the only marking of his rank, besides the *diame* loop.

But Ronal doubted any could look at this man and not see *king*.

It was there in the way he carried himself, in his eyes. Ageless, full of wisdom, power.

If Ronal was reading the power levels right—an elf's power grew as he aged—the man he was looking at was two millennia, easy.

"*Esri* Matiro," Ronal said when the Elvish King finally turned his gray eyes to Ronal. Lowering his head in deference, he met the king's gaze head on and waited.

If the *Esri* decided he didn't want Ronal in his lands...Ronal was as good as dead. He'd never make it outside the wood before an assassin shot him down and relieved him of the burden of his head.

Matiro smiled, a slow curve of a sensuously carved mouth, and he stepped forward, holding a hand out to

Ronal. "I've waited...centuries," he said quietly, his voice like an angel's horn, deep, smooth and musical. "For this moment."

Ronal quirked a brow and slid Daklin a bland look before returning his eyes to the *Esri*. Matiro was reaching inside the simple black tunic he wore, the threads gleaming like silver. *Diame*, again. His clothes were stitched with threads hammered out of the precious metal. Ronal's eyes widened, and his jaw dropped as what the king was holding was revealed.

His father's seal.

"By the blood," Ronal muttered, his voice rough and uneven. "Where did you get that?"

"I was but a child during the battles our people waged against the others. A mere fifty years old, and searching for adventure, eager to fight in the battles against the vicious vampires, who thought to move beyond their borders and settle within the kingdoms throughout Mythe," Matiro said, running the silver links through his fingers. "I agreed to go on what I later learned was a fool's mission, infiltrating one of the vampire soldiers' camps, taking a hostage.

"It was your father," Matiro said softly. "Caval, The High Lord of Demshe, now known as De Amshe, your realm. I used enchantment and elvish magick to subdue him and spirit him away, and I succeeded, a chance that had been very, very slim.

"But before I could turn him over to my superior, an uncle who had expected me to die, Caval came out of the slumbers and started to speak. I didn't realize that a slumbering vampire was so totally aware of everything around them, as I hid and prayed the vampire legions around me would not find my hiding place.

"And he heard me cursing my uncle. It had been pure anger, pure fear that caused me to do such. But he heard my uncle's name and recognized it and when he sighted me upon awakening, he knew who I was. Their scouts were very, very thorough," Matiro said, a faint smile on his lips.

"You know that your father was the one who initiated the treaty between our people, the one who brought about the end to the wars between elf and vampire," Matiro said, cocking a slim brow.

"I know," Ronal replied. His voice was tight, and the emotion that choked him was threatening to overwhelm him. "But I do not understand how you came to hold my father's seal."

"It was a gift…" Matiro held it up, the silver glinting in the sunlight that shone through the trees, the bloodstone sparkling like liquid fire. "He saved my life. With a simple question… *Why would the Elf King order his only son on a fool's mission?*"

The *Esri* smiled, a sad, bitter smile. "That, I had no answer for. I knew, as I thought it through, how unlikely my success was. I should have been sighted and killed on the spot. My father was a brilliant, insightful man—he would have known this. And one lone prince could not dare to hope to turn the tide of the battle. Not with the small, petty missions I was running, thinking that I was doing something so grand for the realm. I finally admitted to myself that it made no sense."

He sighed, looking weary beyond his years. "Then I had to wonder what my uncle's goals were."

The *Esri* turned his head to the side, staring out into the trees. "It was later when I realized the truth. That the king hadn't ordered me on it. My father hadn't even known I had left to join the battles until it was too late, and Kintrin had already started sending me on these fool's missions. My father's bodyguards hadn't caught up with me when I took your father." He paused for a moment to chuckle. "That is a good thing...they most likely would have killed him and who knows which of our people would have had the foresight he had."

Silence ensued for a long moment. Ronal could hear the liquid call of birds overhead, the dull roar of a waterfall somewhere in the distance, and the king's quiet sigh. "My uncle led people to believe that my father had ordered these missions I was undertaking. But he had known I had come to him in secrecy. For weeks, my father believed I was living in solitude as I mastered my gifts of magick. But Kintrin, my uncle, was telling the elvish armies otherwise."

Ronal saw the echoes of remembered pain in the king's eyes. "He was sending you to your death, knowingly," Ronal said softly. "Was he not?"

"Indeed he was. The vampire scouts had heard of the suicidal prince who took on any and all missions, at the behest of his father. I laughed at your father as he asked me that, and then he stood in silence after he told me the truth, that his scouts had heard the tales of my father sending me on these missions... *Matan is a brave and noble king, sending his only son into battle... The boy will be the end of the wars, and Matan knows thus, but to risk his own son...* I tasted the truth in his worlds. Elves can taste a lie, just as a vampire can scent one."

The silver links puddled in Matiro's hand as he slid the chain from one hand, to the other. The bloodstone gleamed and shimmered, the silver embossing on it untarnished with age.

"It was a day and night before I could accept the truth. I left him bound with magick in the trunk of a dead *nage* tree, where he couldn't call out for help. I moved among my people as a wraith and they were discouraged, thinking I would not return from my last mission. They began to curse my father for risking me, when days earlier Caval's scouts had told him how the elvish people praised the king for his selflessness. And I watched from the shadows, unseen and unheard, as Kintrin came out among the armies and told them how the king was wise, and knew what he must do. If the prince dying was what must happen to win the war, then the king would make that sacrifice."

Matiro smiled, a cold, heartless smile. "My father's bodyguards were not pleased. They had been hiding in the shadows as well, unseen by all, until Kintrin spoke those words. To this day, I do not know where they decided to cast him, but he was given back to the earth that very day. One of the guards told me that he was cursing my father as he was flung into his grave, one of the depthless chasms that mark the Mountain Realm."

Matiro started to pace, his eyes seeing the past as he remembered. "When I returned and took your father from the *nage*, I wanted him dead. My fury at my uncle's betrayal was so vast, I couldn't think beyond the objects of my blame. The vampires. But Caval... Caval had wise eyes, the wisest of any man I have ever known, before or since. He looked at me and said, 'Shall we continue the battles and let your uncle succeed? Or do you wish to end this pointless war?'"

Silence reigned once more, and when Matiro spoke, his voice was a low, throbbing whisper that echoed through Ronal. "Pointless...none had ever called it such. But it was pointless. We had launched a war against the vampires simply because they had the courage to do what we did not, go out and live among the mortals of the world, despite their weakness. They sought to thrive and flourish, to seek happiness and life. And we clung to our realm, to the wood and the mountain, living in solitude."

Lifting his head, staring at Ronal from yards away, the king's eyes glowed silver as tears welled. "Your father saved my life, and the lives of thousands of elfkind. We would not have won the battles against the vampires. We had lived too long fighting individually, never as a unit. He saved our lives, all because he was the one man who had the courage to say what many would not."

Now a grin spread across his face and he crossed the distance between them. Ronal jerked in surprise as the king wrapped his arms around him and held fast. "Never again did I see him, once we worked out the plans and I escorted him to my father. But never did I forget him, either. On the day he left, he told my father to give me this. I've kept it with me always."

Ronal spilled the chain around his neck out into the sunlight as the king slowly released him and stepped back. "It's not as nice as mine," he murmured, forcing a smile as he revealed the seal he wore around his neck, the circular flat bloodstone wrapped with silver filigree. "But I imagine it means a great deal to you. Keep it." He reached out and caught the king's hand, pushing the stone back into it. He squeezed once before letting the king's hand fall away.

Matiro fisted his hand around the stone. "This should be yours, not mine," he said.

"I have one. Keep it. I'd never take back what my father gave as a gift," Ronal said quietly. Then his eyes closed. "'Tis good to speak of him."

Matiro cocked his head. "I grieved when I heard of his death in the battles against the Black Warriors. I've visited his resting place — the lovely place you found for him."

Ronal nodded, his throat tight, unable to speak.

"You are welcome here, within my realm, forever and always, son of Caval. And if ever I can repay what your father gave us, I will," Matiro said softly.

* * * * *

"Well, that was…shocking," Daklin murmured as he escorted his friends to the *sekrine*. His own home had chambers for visitors, and clearings nearby for the 'corn Faryn and his wildling get to roam while they were within the realm. "The *Esri* had long fought against the council's attempts to seek vengeance against the vampire. Now I understand exactly why he fought passionately to let the battles go."

Ronal glanced at Daklin and scowled, "Do I truly have to attend this feast he is preparing?"

"'Tis tradition. And while he would not demand your presence, your absence would discomfit him, I believe," Daklin said with a shrug. "He has asked many, many questions about you. Always, I thought he was trying to gather information about the enemy and I despised him for it, for not trusting me. But 'twas you he wanted to know about, simply you."

The elf sent him a sly glance, grinning wickedly. "He will let the people know of what happened all those years ago. He will not allow you to be disrespected in his lands. I know him well. Once the women of the realm know what a hero you are, you shall have them flocking to you. Nothing a lady of the people loves more than a hero. Even a lowly vampire," Daklin said teasingly.

Ronal scowled. "I am no hero. Let him praise my father, for he deserves it, but I want nothing of it."

Chapter Two

Caetria stared at her father in shock. "I will *not* be his guide within the realm. Let Daklin do it, the bastard seems to care for vampire scum—"

Matiro shot her a cold look that froze her blood, and set her face to flaming with shame, although she didn't fully know why. "Watch how you speak of my guests, daughter mine. I love you, but not even you will escape the king's ire if you anger me. Care you to take vigil in the north with the Ice Maidens?"

He wouldn't... But Caetria changed her mind after meeting his eyes. "Why? Why is the vampire so unlike the others? What makes him worthy of our respect?"

"He is *not* unlike the others," Matiro said passionately, startling her. He so rarely displayed any passion, any heat, anything beyond the quiet, royal personage he had been all her life. "The vampire people are a noble one, unafraid and vibrant, lovers of life. However, he is—unique. You've heard the stories of Caval Demshe, the vampire who dared to enter the realm and seek out an end to the wars."

She gave a jerky nod. "They paint him as a noble man, vampire or not. Though how many of the tales are true, I have to wonder. I do believe he was a just creature, even though he was vampire."

Coolly, her father said, "The tales are all true, perhaps not even touching the surface of the man he was. And that man is Caval's son."

Caetria's face flamed.

Son of the man who had, along with the long-dead *Esri* Matan, ended the wars that had killed thousands upon thousands of elfkind.

Caet was quite certain she would be sick.

She'd insulted the son of the man who was responsible for saving the lives of thousands of elves. And that was a truth not even her kind had managed to manipulate through the years.

Her skin started to feel tight and hot as she recalled how she had insulted him at the paths to the realm and her belly churned with nausea. Swallowing, she whispered, "I must beg forgiveness, of both you and Lord Caval's son."

Matiro narrowed his eyes, studying his daughter's face. Oh, he knew her far too well. After a brief study, he asked, "Bloody hell, what have you done?"

Dropping to one knee, she whispered, "I have insulted him greatly." In stilted tones, she repeated what she had said, and then she waited.

Matiro couldn't stop the laugh that bubbled out of his throat. "That is rich, daughter mine. Vampire scum—I hadn't realized you were as closed-minded as so many of the realm. I'm...disappointed." His eyes landed on her face, somber now, as he approached her. Cupping her chin in his hand, he smiled gently. "Child, do not kneel before me. I cannot bear the sight of it."

As she rose, he kept her chin in hand, then he leaned forward and pressed a gentle kiss to her brow. "Love, you are still so very young," he murmured, shaking his head.

Her mouth opened, but she wisely snapped it shut.

He smiled widely. "Ah...showing some wisdom there, Caet. I am proud of you. But you *are* young. Two centuries is nothing to our kind. And you have been far too sheltered, because of our laws, because of the bigotry our kind has against the outsiders. I should never have allowed this to happen, not with you, who will rule when I am gone," he said, his eyes becoming distant.

"Papa, do not speak so," she admonished, feeling her throat tighten. He did this far too often. "You are young yet, especially for our kind. You will be here ruling the realm for centuries to come."

The look he slid her made her insides go cold and tight. A fond smile crossed his face and he passed his hand down her hair. "Hmmm. Life is ever-changing on us, pet. Ever-changing. And we must change with it." He moved away, linking his hands behind his back. "You must make reparations for the insult you have handed Lord Ronal. He is a fine man, even going just by what your cousin has told us. He is not his father, but I see much of his father in his eyes. It was not well done of you."

Caet lowered her eyes, biting her lips to keep from responding. The mutinous replies wouldn't go over well, especially since she *knew* she was wrong. Any other vampire might well have deserved her scathing remarks, but not the son of Caval.

"Now...what to do?" Matiro murmured as he lowered himself to sit on a long-fallen tree. The vines beneath him mounded as he sat, forming a lovely cushion for his backside and Caet had to bite back a smile. The very mountain would shatter itself at her father's feet to increase his comfort level, she mused.

Lifting her eyes to his, she saw him still watching her, patiently. Shrewdly.

"What?" she asked warily.

He smiled. "Lord Ronal will need a companion while he is here. Daklin, well... I am certain, quite certain, that Daklin doesn't wish to provide a feast for the vampire. Nor does the vampire wish to feed upon a man."

"No," she said flatly, shaking her head. The thick braids plaited near her face rustled, the bells woven into the ends tinkling with her movement. "No."

"He also needs a guide. Their entire group will. Daklin will be spending some time with his family—they shouldn't be tied to their *sekrines*. I had been planning to offer you the chance to guide them, and learn from them. Several of the higher-ranking scouts have already begged for the opportunity. However, I feel, after hearing what you have said, that you are the only one acceptable."

"*No*," she whispered, staring at him desperately, although she already knew his mind was made up. The *Esri* had spoken. "You can't possibly mean for me to be his...his...his *whore* while he is here."

Matiro's eyes narrowed.

"And *that* is exactly why it is to be you," he decreed. "It is time you stopped being such a blind little fool and learn something about the world outside your own."

He rose, striding past her quickly.

Caet stood there, shaking, her belly roiling, nausea burning hot and bright through her.

Then Matiro was back at her side and she looked up, startled.

His eyes were glowing and full of fury. "And I would *never* ask my daughter to whore for *anybody*," he said flatly.

In his eyes, she saw the echo of the pain she had unwittingly caused.

Her lids closed and her shoulders slumped.

Damn it all.

* * * * *

Ronal didn't believe he had ever seen a more reluctant guide in all his life.

Not that she wasn't...delicious, he couldn't help but notice that.

She was. Lovely, lithe, with a luminous beauty only seen among the elfkind. Her skin fair glowed, and the flaxen length of her hair was the color of sunbeams and moonlight, all tumbled together.

She met his eyes levelly, and he had to admire that, for he could see her cheeks flushing under his stare. Those purple eyes were the color of gems and they reflected her dislike of him quite clearly.

He wondered...what would they look like fogged by passion?

"My daughter, Caetria. She will be your guide while you visit within the realm," Matiro was saying to them all.

Well, the Elf King's daughter. There goes that idea...even if he ever could persuade her to let go of that damned bloody distrust. For a moment, that was all he could think of, as the rest of the king's words circled meaninglessly in his head.

Finally, the *Esri*'s word penetrated Ronal's thoughts. Ronal nodded slowly. Oftentimes, a leader had their offspring act as a guide. It was a symbol of trust. But then the Elf King's eyes slid to Ronal's and he inclined his head, beckoning Ronal over.

Oh, hell. He couldn't stop the devilish glint that lit his eyes, although he did manage to keep from smiling. Surely he wouldn't give his daughter to Ronal for a vessel, would he?

He would.

"Caet is to be your companion, as well, Ronal," Matiro said quietly, lowering his voice, even though all knew what was being discussed. Ronal was, after all, a vampire. And he had left without a retinue, which meant if he wanted to feed, which he did, he had to find a vessel, or feed from animal prey.

"I had planned to hunt the wood, *Esri*," Ronal said, shaking his head. Although he'd love a chance to sip from that lovely pale neck, he wasn't about to take an unwilling female in his arms. Not even for a simple feeding.

"No. I refuse to allow an honored guest to chase after game," Matiro said flatly, his eyes commanding.

Ronal lifted his chin and replied in a cool, calm voice, "And I refuse to take my sustenance from one who is clearly…unwilling. I'd no more rape a woman than I would feed from a woman who didn't wish it."

"Why would any woman wish such a thing?"

The words seemed to come from her before she could stop them, and Ronal couldn't help but laugh inside as she flushed a lovely shade of red.

Her father cocked a brow and smiled slowly. "Please, tell us, Ronal. Why would any woman wish such?"

A bark of laughter erupted from him, and before he knew it, he was bent double with peals of laughter. "No…no," he muttered, shaking his head once he could breathe. "I will not discuss that in front of a woman and her father."

Her cheeks flushed and that stubborn, soft little chin lifted.

Ronal laughed again, unable to help it. "My lady, forgive me. I am not laughing at you — exactly."

Turning on his heel, he walked away, still chuckling as he joined Daklin at the grandly set table under the treetops. Pepper sat across from him, staring around her with wide eyes, her fingers worrying the necklace that hung between her pretty little breasts. Arys kept running a hand through her tumbled red curls, his eyes so full of wonder and love that it was nearly embarrassing to look at them. The looks that passed between them should be private.

Love that naked…should it be so open like that? Ronal wondered.

In all his years, he had never experienced it. Never even came close.

"You look quite amazed, *chira*," Ronal said, catching Pepper's eyes and smiling. Those odd, mismatched eyes met his and she smiled, dimpling charmingly.

"This place is…amazing," she said, grinning. That gamine grin made her nose crinkle and it was an infectious smile, one that had Ronal smile in return. Her eyes dropped to study his mouth for the briefest of seconds and then she jerked her gaze away, her cheeks flushing red. "Like something out of a dream."

Her gaze wandered to the treetops and the sunlight that filtered in and a frown marred her smooth forehead. Ronal could see the unasked questions in those eyes. Sliding Arys a narrow look, he said in silent communication, *You could just tell her all she wished to know.*

The wineglass in the satyr's hand fell to the table and Arys started to choke on the rich vintage, seizing a cloth and holding it to his mouth as he sputtered. His large eyes slid to Ronal, and the vampire could see the mirth there as the satyr gasped for air. *No, you could answer her questions for a millennium and never tell her all she wished to know. Her curiosity is endless. She makes my kind seem boring*, Arys replied.

Pepper's eyes slid between the two of them and then one red brow arched up. "Poor thing," she cooed, reaching over and patting on Arys' damp chest with a heavy square of silk, soaking up the drops of wine. "I didn't realize you were a klutz."

And then she managed to spill her wine into his lap. With a grin, she spun around and rose, strolling away from the table and disappearing into the trees, calling over her shoulder, "One of these days, Arys, my man, you're going to remember, I do not like being talked about. Not unless I'm invited to join in on the conversation."

Ronal hid his grin behind his hand.

She was an adorable thing; he had to give her that.

And Arys was staring after her with eyes that kept going between frustration and adoration.

Not once had Ronal seen pain or loneliness in the satyr's dark, fathomless gaze. Which made Pepper a rather magickal creature, all in all.

* * * * *

Caet stormed into the clearing, ready to indulge in a long, hot soak, and a long-overdue sulk, only to be brought up short when she saw the red-haired mortal already neck-deep in her family's private pool. Her mouth flattened into a firm, flat line and she decided she would wring Daklin's neck.

Daklin had shown her here. No other way she would have found it. As the woman lifted wide, friendly eyes, Caet blanked her features and forced her mouth into a friendly smile. "Enjoying the pool?" she asked, keeping her voice even.

Pepper smiled, but it was a chilled one. "I'm sorry. I didn't realize I wasn't allowed here," she said, her tongue moving slowly, awkwardly around the trade tongue Caet had used. Getting out of the pool, Pepper reached for her robe.

Caet froze. *Damn it, what in the hell did I do now?* She reached out, laying a cautious hand on the woman's arm and then she knew damned good and well what she had done. The woman was gifted. But so powerful, so well-trained, her shields were all but hidden, and hidden well enough that until Caet had laid hands on her, she hadn't even seen them.

And the mortal witch Pepper had sensed every rotten thought that had rolled through Caet's mind as Caet entered the clearing. The self-deprecating smile that curved her lips was a real one, and the color that flooded her cheeks was real as well. "I am sorry — that was unkind of me, *avri*," she said, lowering her head, touching the tips of her fingers to her temple in a gesture of apology, although the mortal wouldn't understand it. "I am having…a bad day, I believe you would call it."

Pepper stilled, and when Caet looked into her odd, mismatched eyes, she saw a keen intelligence, and an understanding that had her wanting to shift on her feet. "You do not like Ronal. Is it him? Or everybody like him?" she asked.

Caet pressed her lips together. "That is none of your concern," she said arrogantly.

Pepper shrugged, tying the robe more securely at her waist. "I guess not. But your prejudice against him will carry across to your people. Not a wise way for a leader to act," she said softly.

She walked away, moving rather quietly for a mortal.

Caet sighed and dropped down by the edge of the pool, staring into the luminescent surface of the water. It glowed green, reflecting her face back at her as she sat there.

Night was falling, and so far, all she had done today was alienate people, and make those who mattered angry.

"I do believe this day would be better if it just ended," she murmured, reaching out and striking her reflection, watching as her face broke apart and rippled slowly back together.

Hours later, she rose from the soaking pool and dressed, wearing a robe one of the pixes had brought.

A pix was a wonderful creature. A cousin to the very mischievous pixie race, but in every way the pixies' opposite, the pix had settled in with the elves long ago, far too weak to survive alone against the wild magicked creatures that roamed the wood, but determined not to die out. They had made it their life's goal to serve the elves.

And the elves in turn provided for the pix. They protected the smaller creatures, kept the evil in the world from feasting upon them and destroying them.

It was a rather nice symbiotic relationship. Caet's personal pix was a demanding, loveable little creature, barely five feet tall, with vibrant purple hair and eyes the color of starlight. She was a wonderful cook, a talented seamstress, and she was one of Caet's dearest friends.

It looked like she was also rather put out at Caet. Just like everybody else, it seemed.

When Caet called out, "Vay?" she was ignored.

Normally Vay would flutter into view, her wings moving far too fast for Caet to be able to see the lovely mosaic pattern on them. Damn it, Caet wanted some company tonight.

Sighing, Caet started down the path that led to her *sekrine*.

Tomorrow.

Damn it, tomorrow, I'll be nicer to the bloody vampire, even if it kills me.

She rounded the corner in the path, her mind made up, and then she promptly froze in her steps. Her sharp nose caught the scents before her eyes made sense of what she was seeing. Heady female desire, hot male hunger.

It was the vampire, and in his arms he held a woman, her torso bent back over his arm as he ran one wide-palmed hand down the center of her chest. He moved off center, cupping a small, firm breast, circling over the nipple with his finger, pinching it lightly before he bent down and bit it.

Caet felt her own nipples tighten in response. Her belly heated as she watched.

A soft, breathy moan rent the air and a voice, a very familiar one, moaned his name. "Ronal, please...you make me weak," Vay moaned.

A flash of purple and white moved as Vay's wings started to slowly fan the air as Ronal lifted her up, lowering his head to nuzzle her neck. She whimpered and said, "Please—do it. I've heard…magickal things."

Vay's soft, breathy voice hit Caet like a splash of cold water and she cleared her throat.

"Magickal things," Caet repeated as Ronal lifted his head, staring at her from under a fringe of lashes as he licked a slow, lingering trail off Vay's shoulder before he let the pix go. Vay's hands clutched at him as she blinked slowly, still staring at him, confusion in her eyes.

"Vay, my pretty little pix," he murmured, lowering his lips to her ear. "We have company."

"What kind of magickal things?" Caet asked quizzically, arching a brow.

Her eyes roamed over the length of Ronal's body and even in the dark, she couldn't miss the signs of a hungry, aroused man. Her belly quivered and her heart pitched inside her chest, but she refused to admit it was jealousy. No, this was a vampire. Caval's son or not. Still a vampire.

Vay's eyes cleared and she smiled dreamily at Caet, her high, breathy voice trembling as she said, "*Esria* Caeti, ah, magick. A vampire has more magick in his hands than any elfin or pixish lover could ever hope to find, or so I've heard," she whispered, leaning against Ronal, stroking her hand down his chest. "And I'm going to find out…"

"No, sweet," Ronal murmured, shaking his head. "Not tonight." He slid Caet a telling look. "I'm afraid I don't care to be accused of hypnosis of coercion or anything else that might be running through your lady's lovely, but rather narrow, mind."

Vay's lower lip, as purple as her hair, poked out. "But I thought…and you're hungry." Her body shuddered as she rested her hands on Ronal's chest. "Your body almost aches with hunger. It calls me."

Caet watched, feeling like a damned bloody voyeur, as Ronal took Vay's hands and lifted them to his lips. "Aye, sweet. I know. But I've no wish to make your lady unhappy, and this would."

Vay's mouth flattened out. "Fine," she said, her voice rising. "Then make the pix unhappy. All I wanted to do was *help*."

They were left standing there with eyes that watered as Vay exploded in a flash of violet light, pix dust lingering all around them, as her smaller form flew away into the trees.

"Vay!" Caet called, staring at the sparkling trail of violet dust in the trees.

But she was ignored, exactly as she had expected to be.

Lowering her eyes, she flopped to the ground, the vines and flowers mounding together to catch her only seconds before she would have landed on the hard, rock-strewn path. "Damn it," she muttered.

She could feel the vampire watching her, and she closed her eyes, just wishing he would go away. That the entire wood would just go away and leave her be.

"A bit of a spoiled thing, aren't you?" Ronal finally murmured.

Lifting her eyes, she stared at him. "If you please, *betecai*," she forced out the word for honored guest over a reluctant tongue, "I would rather just be alone."

Ronal smiled, his grin white in the darkness. "That was all we wished, as well," he returned.

"Then maybe a public path was not the place for your lovemaking," she said through gritted teeth.

Ronal smiled and said, "Ahhh…well, that is some improvement. At least you consider me, a lowly vampire, capable of making love." He knelt in front of her, leaning until he was nose to nose with her and she could feel the heat radiating from his lean, powerful body. That heat was seductive, and his eyes, those deep green eyes, seemed to hold hers captive as he purred, "And here I thought I was just a beast, capable only of rutting."

He reached out, placed his finger between her brows and stroked. "A lady as lovely as you should not spend so much time unhappy, Caetria," he whispered.

Before she could respond to that, he was gone.

And she hadn't even seen him leave.

Damn, and she thought the elvish warriors could move fast.

Vay was there in the morning, but she was sulking.

"He is *hungry*," Vay said, her high, warbling voice resonating in Caet's head. "It gnaws at me, like a hunger of my own. And I went to him, thinking only to soothe that."

Caet stared at Vay, seeing the pout in the pix's eyes. "Damn it, just go find him and fuck him for crying out loud," she finally snapped. "Feed him while you're at it."

Vay was a sensitive, born of the earth, with a moderate gift of Healing. Anything in pain or suffering was enough to affect her, and the closer the being was, the harder it hit her. Vay was so volatile, her shielding abilities were nil, unless she was in Caet's *sekrine*. When she was outside, she was hit by rampant emotion, and also subject to random visions that sometimes came to fruition.

In short, Vay was a pain in the ass.

Vay flounced over to the lounge and flopped down. "I cannot," she announced. "When he looked at you, I felt something else and I cannot do anything about him now. But if he doesn't feed soon, it will make him ill. And I do not tolerate ill well, you know that." Her silver eyes slid over her shoulder and pinned Caet in place.

"Well, what in the hell do you want me to do?" Caet demanded of her friend. She wouldn't get any rest until Vay had gotten her way.

"Go feed him," Vay said, smiling mischievously. "If you hadn't interrupted then I could leave here without feeling him. So *your* fault. Fix it."

Feed him. Caet's body shivered as Vay's words sank him.

Vay smiled, her purple lips, the color of a summer violet in bloom, curving as she studied Caet's face. "'Tis not what you think. Not what you think—you elves be such blind, bigoted creatures at times," Vay said, rolling to her back and kicking her legs around, rising in a slow easy motion. Her wings started to fan the air. "He is vampire. Just his race—like I am pix, and you are elf."

"He feeds off the blood of others," Caet said flatly.

"*Acha*," Vay agreed, nodding, her springy purple curls dancing around her tawny face. "He does. Born that way! Does that make him evil? A *lachretigre* is born a predator, wanting nothing more than to hunt and hunt. Does that make him evil?"

Vay leaned up on her toes, staring at Caet as the pix whispered in dulcet tones, "No. But it does make the *lachretigre* deadly. And the *tigres* care little about who they hunt, or what lives they destroy, and they take the whole bloody piece of meat, not just a few sips of blood."

She settled back on her dainty feet and sauntered around the room. With a few powerful beats of her wings, she flew up to settle on an exposed beam, staring down at Caet's tight face with a whimsical smile. "Now, the vampire people, they have mind, soul. They do not hunt people, unless they are evil. And Ronal's people track down those who do such. The vampire take only what they need," she said. "So are they evil?"

Caet narrowed her pale lavender eyes, her gaze hard as *diame*, and every bit as icy as the ground in which the precious metal was mined. "You are a wretched, awful thing, you bloody pix," she said, her voice tired. Then she turned and walked away.

She was down the path by the time Vay's laughter bubbled out. Damned bloody pix—making her think, making her question... Of all the people she knew, Vay was the least likely to be fooled by a handsome face. The vampire could have been a haggard creature and still Vay would have been dying to find some way to ease his hunger, all because she couldn't stand for any creature to suffer.

And if Vay, a sensitive, said that the vampire was a good man... Caetria suppressed the growl that rose in her throat. Too much thinking, too early in the morning.

Back at the *sekrine*, Vay snickered, knowing exactly what now troubled her lady's mind. And why.

"Oh, you'll thank me sooner or later," Vay said, her warbling voice full of mirth. A slight hint of jealousy edged its way in and she added, "Maybe someday I will forgive you for costing me last night."

Then she flew down and started setting the *sekrine* to rights.

Chapter Three

He was a bloody hard creature to find, that was for damned sure, Caet decided, nearly four hours later.

When she did finally find him, he was deep in the wood, high in a tree, staring north.

His eyes were grim, and as he looked down the tree to meet her gaze, she fell back a step. "*Esria* Caetria, you should be back home with your kin," he said solemnly.

She arched a brow. "The wood is my home. From the beginning, where Satyr's Wood falls off all the way to the southern regions where the great oceans and sands begin. All of the wood is my home," she said.

"That is a vast piece of land you call home," he said, returning his gaze to the north. "And what of the east? What of Sanctuary?"

She wrinkled her nose. "That is where the mortals dwell. Outside the wood, beyond our lands, where the mortals live… I do not go there."

"No, but they come here. Your magicks are great, but they are many. Sooner or later, a sorcerer will find the paths into your wood, *Esria*," he said quietly. The setting sun painted his pale skin golden, and he squinted, turning his eyes away from the light.

"I thought vampires couldn't take the light," she said quietly.

"The older a vampire becomes, the more we can take," he said. A weary sigh racked his body. "And I am very old." He lifted his hand and held it out to the sun, watching as the sun shone on it, his eyes blank. "But to the younger of my kind...the sun is death."

Something twisted in her belly at the sound of his voice. She hadn't ever heard anybody so sad, not in her entire life. All two hundred years...and he was almost as old as her father.

"Come down away from the sun's light, *betecai*," she said softly, gazing up the tree that soared two hundred plus feet into the air. "It causes you pain."

He slid her a look, and the distance between them didn't matter at all. Her sharp eyes caught the appraising look in his. She heard the whisper of a sigh and watched as his eyes slid back to the north. She felt something twist her heart and she realized, *He's homesick.*

And he was also suicidal, she decided and she barely had a chance to leap out of the way as he came hurtling down out of the tree, feet first. He landed in front of her, his knees flexed, his long hair settling around his shoulders. He reached up and gathered it into a loose tail, shoving it back off his shoulders. His brows were high and slanting over his dark green eyes, winging up at the edges, drawing attention to those rather amazing eyes.

"Aren't you going to make a cutting remark and stalk away, *Esria*?" he asked coolly, flicking a lock of hair out of his eyes before dusting his hands off. His mouth curved into a wolfish smile, displaying those dazzling teeth.

Taunting her.

She closed her eyes and swallowed. "I have been—dreadfully rude. I offer my most humble apologies," she said, bending at the waist, the ends of her hair sweeping the ground. She held the position for ten seconds, all that was required for the heir to the Crown.

When she rose, she felt his eyes even more intent on her than before and it took all of her composure not to let him see how badly just his presence affected her.

By the glint in his eyes though, she suspected he had some idea.

Inclining her chin, she said, "My father wishes me to act as guide to you and your friends. It would be an honor. And…to be your…companion," she was so proud. She barely stumbled over the word. "It is my duty and my honor to be such."

The smile faded from his mouth and he reached up, tracing a long finger down her neck.

She felt the heat of his touch and wondered at it. She had always thought a vampire was a cold, dead creature, reanimated by some dark evil magick and fueled by the blood he stole from the unwilling.

But he was warmth, and he was life.

And try as she might, she could sense no darkness, no evil inside him. If truly he was the monstrous creature she had always imagined vampires to be…wouldn't she sense that evil within him?

Something passed through his eyes and his face tightened, a hunger moving across his features.

She tensed, preparing herself.

But Ronal only lowered his head and murmured against her ear, "I take no woman unwillingly."

And then he slid away, his fingers grazing her cheek as he passed.

For the longest time, she could feel the heat of his touch. And it took her several long moments to figure out that he had refused what she had offered. It took even longer than that to figure out that the vague, empty feeling in her belly was disappointment.

* * * * *

Ronal clenched his jaw as the musk of her hungry body floated to him on the air as he roamed the wood. It would have taken less than five minutes—and then she wouldn't have been unwilling.

With that flaxen hair and those amethyst eyes… Damnation, there was very little he had wanted in recent memory quite as much as he wanted a taste of her. And not just that pale, swan-like neck either. Her mouth, and that long slender body.

And that haughty attitude of hers. Damned if he didn't like her. Even if she was a bigoted, little spoiled brat. She had been exposed to negativity and hatred against his kind all her life. Her father had been silent against it for the most part, ignoring it, expressing his displeasure simply through his silence, as he waited for a chance to show them they were wrong.

Ronal wondered if Matiro had been waiting, all this time, for Ronal to come.

The elves were such an odd lot.

He wouldn't be surprised if the *Esri* had been given a vision saying the vampire would come, and thus the Elf King had simply waited.

Ronal just wished the *Esri* would keep his damnable, tempting child away from him. She was too young, too innocent, too sweet…and she hated his kind. Even though she had been a little more approachable today, he wouldn't fool himself into thinking she would be a willing vessel. Not for his hunger.

And not for his lusts either.

He'd be better off finding the pretty little pix from last night. Or a more receptive elf. He had already seen not all were of the mind of the king's heir. His footsteps were even leading him down the path where he could just barely distinguish the unique scent of the pix.

But then...*darkness, foul and black.*

Black lightning came splitting down out of the sky, renting the air, filling it with an acrid stench. It struck something, miles away from where Ronal stood, but he didn't remain on the ground. His lesson last time was still too fresh in his mind, and he knew how fast the black lightning could amass for a second strike.

Ronal leaped from the ground, taking flight and alighting in a tree hundreds of feet off the ground. His eyes went to the north and he tracked his people. *Safe, m'lord...* Sadeisha replied as he felt the Lord's touch on his mind. Nothing else, no sign or sound of disturbance, so Ronal withdrew his touch and turned his focus to the wood.

For *there* was the disturbance.

None was serious. Not to Ronal's eyes. But the fae were...shaken. None had breached their barriers in centuries.

Even from his perch, miles away, he could feel their distress.

* * * * *

He walked into the *Esri*'s home, a lush, rich *sekrine* that seemed more an extension of the wood than an actual indoor dwelling. The carved inlay of the walls gleamed and light came from nowhere. Under his feet, the stone floor was warm and far softer than a floor made of stone should be.

Matiro was sitting in a carved wooden chair speaking quietly with Daklin. At his feet, Caet was sitting, one knee drawn up to her chest, as she listened, her eyes dark and stormy.

Cray was standing by the window, his wings spread wide, his stance stiff, anger in every line of his body.

Arys was seated on the floor and Pepper was pacing in tight circles around the *sekrine*. She kept reaching up and running her hands through her hair, muttering to herself.

When Ronal crossed the threshold, all eyes moved to him and he arched a brow.

"Yes?"

Daklin growled, "You are determined to drive us mad with worry, aren't you, you old bastard?" Moving away from the Elf King, the enchanter got into Ronal's face and said, "Always, you must be alone. Never take another living soul with you, leaving your friends to worry sick about you."

"Well, it leaves fewer dead bodies that way," Ronal drawled. Then he grinned rakishly and grabbed Daklin by his long ears, jerking the startled elf closer and planting a smacking kiss on his mouth. "Daklin, my friend. I didn't know you cared so much."

He whirled away, laughing, as Daklin stared at him, bemused, rubbing the back of his hand across his mouth. "You're insane, vampire, you know that, don't you?"

"He's vampire, so of course he's insane," Cray said from the window, flicking them a glance from over his shoulder. "But you're elf. That makes you even more so."

Matiro chuckled. He looked at Ronal, his weary eyes lit with relief. "I am glad to see you are unharmed. We felt the bolt cut through the shields, and even though it was weakening, just by powering through our barriers, I worried. It struck nothing—I cannot even say if it had a true target. None can see inside my people's lands. They may use force and magick to throw something at us, but actually see within our lands? That cannot happen...at least not yet," Matiro said, a sigh escaping his lips. "Our shields finally succeeded in stopping it. This time. But what of the next?"

"A target, no," Ronal said quietly. "A goal, yes. But they may have succeeded. Perhaps their goal was to make your people afraid."

"Elves do not fear mortal magick," Caet said softly from the floor.

"Then you are not a very wise people."

All eyes turned to Pepper.

Her face flushed, but she swallowed and said, "Arys has been telling me of the world here. It sounds...not so very different from mine. Much more magickal." She slid her lover a look, her hand came up to rest on his shoulder, and his hand covered hers, squeezing it. "But not so very different. It has its prejudices, its hatreds. It's had its wars. Different races. And humans who are exactly like me. Mortals," she repeated, mimicking Caet's tone.

Inclining and shaking her head, she said, "The mortals outnumber every other race on this planet. There's no Census Bureau, no polls going around, but I'd say humans are the vast majority."

Everybody frowned a little at her wording and a few sent Arys telling glances to which he only shrugged.

Pepper continued. "Humans are survivors, Caet. We're stubborn, and we can be stupid, and loud, sometimes obnoxiously so. But just because we don't live hundreds of years, that is no reason to dismiss us," she said softly.

Caet gently said, "Mortal magick is weak."

Pepper smiled. A very chilly smile. "Really? I'll remember that, the next time I feel that black lightning coming out of nowhere. And I'll let you deal with it alone," the weak little mortal witch said. She turned to Arys and leaned down, murmuring into his ear.

He started to rise, but she shook her head, rather adamantly.

The satyr sighed and lowered himself back down, but his gaze spoke volumes to the human and she rolled her mismatched eyes, but nodded. She stalked off, her shoulders held rigid with temper, her entire body stiff with it.

Daklin waited until Pepper was outside and moving away before he looked at Caet. "You know, I don't recall you being such a foolish thing," he said to his cousin. "How can a few decades change a woman so?"

Caet lifted a brow and calmly said, "Human magick is too weak for me to be concerned about."

Daklin threw the pewter goblet he held in his hand, the loud clang it made on the table startling Caet. Her eyes leaped to his and she blinked at the fury in his gaze. "It's a bloody mortal who is most likely behind all of this!" he bellowed. "That witch you just insulted is a mortal. She knows magick better than any being I've ever met in my life, mortal, fae or other. She says it is no vampire, no elf and nothing else she has met since she fell through the blasted Gate.

"That leaves a *mortal*, dear cousin," Daklin finished, his voice dropping to a furious hiss. He stalked over and crouched down in front of her. "And that magick wasn't weakened by the shielding we are so bloody proud of. It was *stopped*. Not by your shields as your father thinks. By *her*. A *mortal*. Again."

Caet pulled back from Daklin, shaken. Gone was the lighthearted, playful cousin she knew. In his place was a warrior, and he had thoroughly distressed her although she would never admit it.

"Daklin, what you are talking about?" Matiro asked, reaching out a hand and laying it on Caet's shoulder. "And be mindful. That is *my* child you are ranting at. Have a care you do not go too far."

"Your child should have a care. She is not a babe in the wood, not any longer. But she persists in acting like one and it grows tiresome. She insults Ronal at every turn," Daklin growled, rising, his eyes stormy, his voice deep and thunderous.

Ronal moved forward and caught Daklin by the arm. No words were spoken aloud, but they were spoken nonetheless.

Daklin's eyes narrowed and he jerked his arm from Ronal, turning to face Matiro, angling his chin up arrogantly. "The vampire can go hump a stake sideways,

for all I bloody care. I care little if he doesn't take offense—
I have taken offense. She belittles Pepper. That is the
second insult. So now she has insulted not just one friend,
but two."

Cray sighed from the corner. "Daklin, she is young."

Daklin's head whirled, his braids flying out, the bells
on the tips ringing merrily. "That does not matter. She will
one day be queen. She is *Esria*, heir to the throne. She
should already be showing wisdom," Daklin said coldly.
"So I will tell her what the four of us already know."

He stalked over and knelt in front of Caet and she
wished she could just sink into the floor. Because she had a
very bad feeling she wasn't done apologizing for the day.
She had messed up.

Again.

"The little witch you just insulted, you remember, the
mortal witch, with the weak mortal magick?" Daklin asked.
He flicked a glance over her shoulder at her father. "She
just saved the lives of untold elves. If the black lightning
had come and she had not shielded, it would have
shattered through the enchantment shields we use, and it
would have decimated all within the area."

"Our protections have lasted for millennia," Matiro
said, the calm, serene mask cracking, his gray eyes
swirling as he rose and glared at Daklin.

"If you don't believe me, then check for the presence
of the wards," Daklin said. "I already have. They *are not
there*."

A soft sob escaped Caet's lips as she tried to do just
that. The ever-present glow of the shielding that had so
long surrounded her people was just…gone. And Caet felt

what seemed like the very foundations of her world start to crack…

"Da…what are we going to do?"

"Wanted to speak with you, *Esri*, my beloved did," Arys said, his deep, silken voice somber. He lifted his gaze from the table and met the Elf King's eyes. "And this is why. Rebuild your shielding, she will help. She is—angry. But she will return, once she has ahhh…chilled? Her words are so strange."

Ronal chuckled, settling onto the stool across from the satyr. "I like your mate, Arys. She is…unique. And I agree with Cray. A warrior witch, like those of old," he murmured.

"Pretty mine," Arys murmured, cocking his head, as though hearing her from afar. He winced. "She is…ah, eloquent in her anger." At Ronal's arched brow, Arys tapped his brow. "I cannot block her thoughts from mine. But that is not a troublesome thing. Her thoughts are…ever interesting."

Across from them, Daklin was staring out the window, his stance stiff, his eyes wintry. *He is being rather hard on the youngling*, Ronal said silently.

Arys shrugged. *She will lead the People of the Wood one day. And I have an unhappy thought that it will be sooner than she likes. She is…not prepared to lead them. And I do not think she wants to. Daklin will not see his people fail because she persists in acting like a child.*

Ronal slid his gaze back to the satyr, meeting those dark, wise eyes. Too bad the satyr would never leave his wood. He had a heart that would do good for many, if he would but find it in himself to lead. *What have you seen?* he asked.

I am no viseur, Arys said, his eyes growing distant, his gaze dropping to his palms. One black nail started to make circles on his other palm and Ronal suspected no matter what Arys claimed, he was indeed seeing *something*. *I have no gift of foresight. But the Elf King has the cloud of death on him. It follows him everywhere he walks. Death is stalking him.*

Have you told Daklin?

Arys lifted his lashes. *If I tell Daklin, I will lose a friend. He must be here to help lead them, for a time. Caetria is not ready. I do not know if she ever will be. And if Daklin knows, Daklin will die trying to save him — and the Elf King will still die.*

Ronal felt his heart sink to his belly as he thought of the light that lit the serene king forever going out.

And Caet, that lovely, winsome creature, the pain in her eyes...his throat tightened.

From behind them, the fallen one approached. Cray bent his head low enough to whisper, "We cannot change what is to come, though we may be able to save some of them. But not if we let ourselves be ripped asunder. Pay attention."

Arys blinked, his lashes lowering to hide the surprise in his eyes. The satyr nodded and turned away, rising from his seat to move over to the elf. As he moved away, he said privately to Ronal, *I spoke of this to no one before I spoke to you...just now.*

Ronal slid the winged man before him an appraising look.

So how had Cray known?

Cray's storm cloud eyes revealed nothing.

* * * * *

Leagues away, a wizened figure stood before a mirror, his face twisted with hatred. He had failed.

Again.

He turned and spat in an urn before pacing around the room, muttering to himself. "Damned fae," he rasped. "Damn their shielding."

But it should have worked.

The fae's shielding was millennia old. Time alone should have eroded enough, so that if he hit that one spot, it *should* have shattered, and he *should* have hit his targets.

Matiro and Caetria should be dead. And the People of the Wood should be weak, weak enough that his followers could slide in, spirit away enough of the weaker elves, enough for a harvesting.

His eyes landed on the proud, arrogant man standing beside the arched doorway. "Your calculations failed," he hissed.

"Something else interfered," Remero said smoothly, shrugging his shoulders. It had been a year and half since his "disappearance" and he had prospered here. And quite well. His calculations had been on the mark. But something had slid in, some shielding that wasn't of elvish magick. He had felt it before. Only six weeks ago.

"Something else?" the master shrieked, whirling and sweeping one arm across a worktable, clearing it of vials and potions and goblets. Smoke and fumes filled the air and Remero started to breathe shallowly from his mouth.

"Aye, something else. We felt it before, the day you attempted to kill the Gatekeepers," he said, reminding his master of that day.

"Ah, yes, your other failure," the master said, his face going florid with hatred.

Remero blinked and wondered if maybe he should have kept his mouth shut.

"What is it? What is blocking me? Shielding them? How can it sense me?" he muttered, ignoring Remero completely as he started to pace, tugging at his white hair.

Across from them, a young woman lay huddled in a cage, trembling with terror, her eyes wide, her chest heaving as she sobbed. Stupid thing. She was still breathing through her swollen nose.

And the fumes from the potions on the floor were getting to her.

Remero could scent the damiana and he bit back a smile.

Maybe, just maybe, he could get the master to let him have her. She wasn't much use to them magickally anyway. Not anymore.

But her death...that just might bring them some energy. And in a few minutes, she'd feel like being fucked to death.

Remero would be more than happy to oblige.

Chapter Four

Caet stood stiff and still, her back braced against the tree trunk. From here, the damage was impossible to miss. By the Father, if the mortal hadn't shielded, many would be dead.

How could I have been so very wrong? Granted, she had never met a mortal before…but mortals had always been known to be the lesser species in the world.

Known by whom? a tiny little voice within her head asked.

Caet scowled. She wanted, badly, to silence that voice, the one that had been whispering gently to her ever since Vay, with but a few simple words, had derailed her so easily this morning.

*Born that way…*Vay had said. And why had he been born that way? Because some power had wanted him born that way. He had been meant, from the beginning of time, to be born vampire.

So…did that make him evil? A monster? *Vampire scum…?*

Caet simply didn't know what to think any more. But she did know that when she looked into his eyes, everything inside her stilled. And then her heart would start to slam against her chest and her belly would tighten. She had faced evil before…and evil had never made her feel like this.

She closed her eyes and took a deep breath, trying desperately to center and focus her thoughts. So much trouble in the air around them, so much chaos.

Opening her eyes, she stared back out over the wood of Glynmare Forest, her people's home, and felt her gut tighten as she saw the line of destruction.

Ronal had been inside the line when the lightning had come down, so he had missed being hit and Pepper's shield had shunted the energy around and into the ground.

But what hadn't hit the shield had struck the trees and the earth surrounding them.

It looked like a storm of flaming rock had fallen from the skies. Trees were blackened, some with branches broken. Some were smashed.

Some were gone altogether, nothing but ashes.

"What if people had been around here when it hit?" Matiro asked, his voice flat.

Arys said softly, "Pepper has a—sensing, if you will. Where to stop the shielding, she knew. 'Tis not perfect, but 'twas the best she could do."

Matiro sighed. "That wasn't what I meant. I owe her much, satyr. But if it happens again, we cannot rely on the powers of a woman who is not one of us. We cannot expect her to remain among us always. And what about the next time?" The glimmering diamond-like shine of his *diame* crown seemed to weigh very heavily on his brow at that moment, as he wrapped a hand around a thick branch and leaned out from the tree, staring down over hundreds of feet at his wood.

"You have sorcerers among you," Ronal said from his perch several branches up.

Caet slid him a glance. His feet rested lightly in the tree and he looked as at home as an owl would.

Matiro lifted a brow and said, "Yes."

Ronal chuckled dryly. The wind blew, whistling through the branches, blowing the black silk of his hair across his face. Lifting his face to the fading sunset, he said, "Bring them here. I know the elvish sorcerers tend to wander away and live in solitude. But call them back. Use them. Their magick will equal his, can fight it. They will understand his magick better than the enchanters will."

Matiro's lips flattened into a grim, straight line. "Elvish sorcery is too deadly, Ronal. It drives them near insanity," he said, shaking his head. "'Tis almost an evil thing, elvish sorcery."

Yes, sorcery drove their kind mad. But it wasn't just elvish kind. It was the same for any long-lived race. Sorcery was unlike witchcraft, which channeled through the earth into you. With sorcery, one had to tap into the otherworld to use it, and that eventually would drive one mad, unless one just had a very, very strong will.

And it was unlike Enchantment, which coerced the elements into behaving in a way unnatural to them, for a certain amount of time.

Sorcery was deadly.

It was evil, in her opinion.

And it had taken too much from them.

Caet rubbed her hands up and down her arms, chilled as she listened to them.

Her eyes moved to Ronal's face. He was studying her father with something akin to pity. *Oh, Da will hate you for that, vampire. He doesn't want your pity.*

"It's taken somebody from you before, hasn't it?" Ronal asked quietly.

Matiro's eyes closed. Caet had to stifle a whimper. Daklin said quietly, "Her mother, Ronal. She left them long ago. I do not know if she ever gave up the battle or not."

Ronal's gentle, "I'm sorry," had Matiro nodding. Caet just stared at him, blinking rapidly to keep the tears from falling. She wouldn't cry, damn it. Not over a mother she hadn't seen since she was a teenaged child. "I am sorrier than you will ever know. But I've seen elves who can walk in the world of power and not lose themselves. One of the most powerful beings I've ever met is an elvish sorceress, the Lady of the White, a woman with a talent for appearing in a place just as she is most needed.

"I've met her a number of times over the past few centuries...and she is not evil. There are those who can resist the darker calls of magick. She is proof that it can happen—it takes a strong will, a strong love to anchor them. But it can happen. You must call them to you. If you wish to save your people."

Caet flinched. Hadn't they been enough to anchor her mother? Of course not—otherwise Asmine would still be with them.

Cray was flying in lazy circles around the trees and now he stopped, hovering before them, staring at Matiro, his eyes somber. Caet felt her heart trip inside her chest. There was something almost...hypnotic about that man's gaze. Her eyes moved to the wings, so unlike the wings of pixes and pixies. Huge, feathered wings taller than the man himself and when spread wide open, they blocked out the sun.

"War is coming upon Mythe, *Esri*. I feel it in my heart. You feel it as well. Creatures as old as we are, we can taste it, almost as we can taste the change of the seasons. Will you see your people falter? Or will you give them hope?" Cray asked, his voice as musical as an elvish kiarharp, deep and throbbing, almost commanding them to listen.

Caet stood there, feeling the rough bark of the ancient oak at her back as she stared at her father, facing the fallen one. Matiro had on a short tunic, belted at his trim waist with woven *diame*, supple leather leggings and boots that rose over his knees. The robe was blue silk, the color of the sky at midnight. Such a dashing, commanding figure, her father was.

And Cray, like a heavenly warrior of old. His wings beat at the air with slow, lazy strokes, the muscles in his naked chest flexing with each stroke. Around his waist, he wore a short kilted skirt. Save for a pair of soft boots that stopped at his knees, he wore nothing else.

Royal, elegant civilization meets ancient raw strength, she thought.

Da will never summon back the sorcerers. They are too uncontrollable, too unpredictable.

But as she watched…he nodded.

Cray crossed one arm across his chest and lowered his head, his black hair falling to hide his face. His body lowered in the air for a moment as his beating wings slowed, and he bowed before the Elf King, then he flew away.

Matiro turned, walking along the branch of the tree like a cat, nimble and light-footed, like all elves. When he reached Caet, he laid his palm against her cheek and said gently, "I will not risk our people to useless death. We must be protected."

And she watched as he began the climb back down, his hands and feet as quick and light as if he hadn't even seen his fifth century.

And he was nearing his fifteenth.

Her eyes filled with tears. *The sorcerers...he's bringing them back...*

She lifted her head and stared into Ronal's eyes for a long second. In his eyes, she saw compassion, and understanding that she hadn't imagined a vampire could ever have.

Without a word, she walked to the end of the nearest branch and leaped.

Ronal flung himself after her, bellowing her name, only to hear Daklin behind him laughing in the trees.

And then her flaxen-haired form swooped away from him as she flung out some silken skein that was attached to a spiked tool. Ronal landed on the ground just in time to see her climbing up the trunk of another forest giant, jerking the tree spike out of it, winding the *diame* rope and tucking the rappelling gear away before she started down another branch.

She leaped, flung the rope, climbed...and was lost from sight.

"What did you think she was going to do, kill herself?"

Yes. For a brief moment, that tortured look in her eyes had scared him senseless.

Looking into Daklin's amused blue eyes, he said pithily, "Why don't you go find some randy goat to fuck?"

Daklin said, "Now you weren't supposed to let my sick secrets out around my people, vampire. And I thought we were friends." Slinging an arm around Ronal's neck, he said, "Besides, I've had fun with that pretty little pix you turned down."

"Vay isn't my type," Ronal said, elbowing Daklin in the gut and moving away.

"She bleeds," Cray said simply, alighting on the ground in front of them and halting them in their tracks.

Ronal lifted his hand and tucked his thumb under his chin, then flipped it at Cray, a silent gesture telling the fallen one where to go. "So do you, you winged bastard, and I'm not likely to seek you for a bedmate," Ronal said dryly.

Cray cracked a grin and looked back toward where the king's daughter had disappeared. "I have an idea why the vampire is not interested in the pix, Daklin, although it may not please you to hear," Cray said, a wicked light appearing in his stormy eyes.

Daklin laughed. "Oh, mercy—the vampire wants to fuck my cousin. I'm shocked, I'm offended...please go and do it, and get it over with. Maybe the child will grow up. Before she gets herself hurt. Or worse," Daklin muttered, shaking his head.

Ronal froze and slid Daklin a narrow look.

"You should really speak of her with a bit more respect," he said quietly. His voice was icy and the air around them literally dropped several degrees.

Daklin felt it and wondered at the rage that had caused it. But he hid his smile, along with his inner glee. Although the vampire was in for a rude awakening if he thought he'd have an easy time with Caetria.

"I should? Why? Because she is heir? That is because she was born to it. Not because she has earned it. Should I speak of her with respect because she has earned my respect? Ten years ago…twenty…I would have. But the woman I have seen of late is a child, a spoiled one who has let the blind views of an isolated people affect her. That is not a woman whom I should speak of with respect. When she acts like the leader I know she can be, then I will speak of her with respect. Until then…"

Daklin shrugged and walked away. Arys was just now dropping down out of the tree and dusting his hands off, staring at them with bemusement. "Cloven feet are not made for climbing trees," he muttered, shaking his head and removing branches and leaves from his sable hair.

He looked at Ronal and arched a brow. "You look like you need to *chill* out," he suggested, grinning.

Ronal, in turn, replied with a saying he had picked up from a refugee he had escorted out of Satyr's Wood. "Bite me, Arys," he said dryly.

And then he stalked off.

Arys lifted a winged brow and said, "Now he is the vampire. Why in the Blessed One's name would I bite him?"

Cray was too busy snickering to respond.

* * * * *

He would call the sorcerers back.

He would call *her mother* back.

Caet sat on the highest limb of the tallest tree she could find, staring into the star-strewn sky, feeling the call of her father.

All would feel his power tonight.

All would answer, save for her. None would be able to resist. Save for her. She knew what he was asking, and she would go back to him. Once she had reconciled herself to the fact that sometime soon, she would have to face the woman who had walked away from her before she had even seen her thirteenth birthday.

But I've seen elves who can walk in the world of power and not lose themselves. It can happen — it takes a strong will, a strong love to anchor them.

Ronal knew elvish sorcerers who could walk in the world of power and not be lost to madness. It took great love, great focus, he'd said. But Matiro and Caet hadn't been important enough.

Caet never once thought that her mama was dead.

They would know.

"I caused you pain earlier," a soft, quiet voice said from behind her.

Caet's heart tripped in her chest and she barely managed to muffle the shriek in her throat. Licking her lips, she gently said, "When a woman is sitting hundreds of feet off the ground, how wise is it to sneak up on her, Ronal?"

He chuckled, a little closer now. "Well, after what you did to me earlier, leaping out of that tree, I figure you deserve a fright. Were I mortal, my heart would have stopped." He appeared on the branch beside her, simply materializing out of thin air and Caet's eyes widened, her heart quivering in her chest, a fine tremor running through her body. He chuckled and leaned in, moving his face along her neck, breathing in. "Rather like yours just did. Did you just have a fright, *avasi*?"

A fright…she wasn't sure if that was what she'd had or not. Having him appear out of thin air hadn't exactly done a lot for her chaotic mind, but suddenly, hot little waves were crashing in her belly.

Damn it all to the lowest levels of hell…she thought as she stared at him. He bothered her. Badly.

Why couldn't he have been what she had expected? A lascivious, evil, soulless creature?

But he was so much more than she had ever imagined possible…

Staring at him made her belly clench with need, made her heart pound, and her blood churn. Her pussy was feeling slick and hot and she was…*hungry*.

Like she hadn't felt in years.

Decades.

She ran her tongue along her lips and whispered, "Exactly what did you just do?" she asked. "How did you appear here? From nowhere?"

He grinned, and Caet couldn't help but notice the even white length of his teeth, or the longer, sharp angle of his eyeteeth. Did he use those…she forced her gaze away from his mouth, meeting the emerald depths of his stare as he said, "It is just a part of what I am. Just like your hair, or your smile…or your fear of seeing your mother again is part of you."

"I am *not* afraid of seeing her again," she hissed, jerking away from him, sliding away from the trunk of the tree, balancing on the limb, her heels tucked underneath her and her eyes glowing furiously in the light. "Do not presume to *know* me. I am not afraid of her. I do not know her. She abandoned me."

Ronal's eyes glimmered oddly as he studied her perched on the tree. "Do you have to sit there perched like a cat?" he asked.

She arched a brow at him, brushing a lock of hair back from her face. "Some legends say that the people descended from the cats," she said, smiling sweetly, looking down at the ground far below. "And you don't seem too concerned if you fall."

"I did not *fall*. I jumped. And my body structure is much denser than yours," he returned.

She laughed, but hooked a hand around the branch overhead. "Relax. Our babes might as well be born in trees," she said, the corners of her lips curling up in a smile. He feared for her safety…that warmed her, for some reason. And provided yet more proof that he wasn't what she had thought a vampire would be. "I walk the trees as well as I walk the paths of the wood. Of course, the trees are usually quieter."

One slanted brow rose higher and he said, "Well, at least you are no longer sitting here grieving and feeling such sadness, the pixies, the pix, even the flowers and the butterflies feel your sorrow."

She shrugged and said, "There are no pixies here. They cannot tolerate their pix cousins. And we like the pix."

Moonlight filtered through, casting his face in silvered light. She could smell him, feel his heat, and she whispered, "I don't know what to think of you."

Ronal whispered back, leaning forward, "Why do you have to think anything of me?"

And then his mouth pressed against hers, his lips warm and tasting of honeymead. That wasn't what she had expected him to taste like. Wind started to whip through the air in a stronger gale as she leaned into him, one hand sliding up to cup the back of his neck, under that thick heavy fall of raven-black hair. His tongue breeched the barrier of her lips, a husky moan rumbling in his throat, making his chest vibrate against her breasts.

Her nipples tingled, started to throb. Fisting her hand in his hair, she whimpered and moved closer against him, sighing when he caught her in his arms, leaned back against the trunk of the tree, and held her snug against his chest as he took her mouth harder.

Sweet…

The word whispered through her mind like a soft caress.

By all that is ancient, you are sweet…

Her body trembled and her head fell back from his so she could stare at him, running her tongue over her lips. "No creature on earth should be able to breech my mind," she whispered. "Elvish are not like mortals."

"And neither are vampires," he said, reaching up and passing his thumb over her lip. "But I have an unfair advantage. The power of the Gate has affected my powers and changed them. They are no longer like the powers of another vampire. And the Pillar Gatekeepers share a bond. My bond with Daklin has augmented my powers even more…and touching you seems to enhance that."

His eyes glowed, casting a faint light as he stared down at her. A soft curse whispered from him and Caet whimpered when his arms caught her tightly against him and then the world started to whirl past her as he leaped from the tree. "What are you—"

Her startled shriek was muffled against his lips as he pressed his mouth against hers in mid-leap, their bodies plummeting to the earth hundreds of feet below. His mouth withdrew from hers only a breath before they landed on the ground and Ronal murmured against her throat, "Now that will just about take your breath away," as he let her body slide to the ground.

Caet's body was quivering, from the rush of adrenaline, from the freefall, but she knew, most of all, from Ronal. His scent flooded her head, and the taste of him, honeymead and male, lingered on her tongue and she wanted *more*. Her nails dug into his shoulders as she stared up at his face. "I think my heart just stopped."

He laughed, his breath caressing, tickling the hair by her ear as he rubbed his cheek against her throat. There was a drugged quality to the sound, almost as if he was hypnotized. He whispered roughly, "No, it beats. I can hear it, feel it—"

And then, almost as suddenly as he had leapt from the tree with her in his arms, he set her from him and he was fifteen feet away, staring at her with wide eyes, his gaze hypnotic.

And his mouth…his fangs had dropped.

"Go away, Caet," he said quietly. He turned on his heel and stared out into the peacefulness of the wood, his body terribly still, unmoving.

Silence had fallen around them.

No birds called, no animals moved, no predators hunted.

Caet realized it was because they sensed a greater one was among them.

Ronal's hunger was growing, but he kept it in check. How long could the predator within him be controlled? Staring at him, sensing the struggle, she suspected he could beat the hunger into submission for a very long time. But he suffered for it.

Damn it all.

He was far too noble for her liking.

Vampires were supposed to be the cold, unfeeling creatures that she had always thought them to be. Not a warm, seductive, creature who made her yearn and want…

"Damn it, Caetria, *go away!*" Ronal roared, whirling, his long black locks flying and settling around his strong featured face as he glared at her. That hunger was there in his eyes now, naked and glowing, as he stared at her. And she suspected he could fight it forever, and he could win. But something about her made it harder.

She smiled. For some reason, that thought pleased her. Reaching up, she untied the laces at her bodice, loosening the leather until she could slide it off. His eyes narrowed, the green glowing so brightly that it cast stark shadows on his cheeks as he stared at her. "What are you doing?" he asked, his voice throbbing.

The lacing on her blouse was easier, and it went from the high, soft neck to her naval, but the shirt was made of silk, not tough leather, so the lacing slid easily through the grommets and she soon had it open to halfway between her breasts, brushing the high collar of the deep violet silk aside, baring her neck. Ronal's eyes stared at the bared flesh of her chest, the narrow strip revealed between the lacings of her blouse, moving up to linger on her neck, to her eyes.

"'Tis not wise to taunt a man dying of thirst," he warned her, his voice low.

She lifted a brow and said, "I'm many things, but outright cruel is something that's never been one of my amusements. Spoiled, short-sighted, close-minded…these things, I am, according to Daklin, and my father as well." A grimace twisted her mouth and she sighed. "But even they know I am not cruel."

Ronal moved forwarded, stalking her like a *pantiere*, one of the giant forest cats, his eyes as green as theirs, more seductive. "No, not cruel at all. But are you sure this is what you want?" he asked, stroking a long finger down the line of her throat.

She shivered under the caress. Her nipples tightened to the point of pain and her belly clenched into a tight, hot little ball of need… *Did she want it?* She really wasn't certain.

But he was suffering. She knew he had hunted while he was in the wood. But whatever he was taking wasn't giving him what he needed. She lifted her eyes to his and smiled, unaware that her fear was written all over her face. "If I wasn't sure, I wouldn't still be standing here," she said honestly. At least *that* much she was sure of.

Well, one other thing…she wanted him. *That* she knew as well.

He moved behind her and wrapped her in his arms, brushed her hand out of the way, and pressed a hot, openmouthed kiss to the exposed arch of her neck. He ran his hands down the outside of her breasts and she shivered, her eyes widening. Her nipples tightened, aching, as something moved through her, insubstantial and mystical, tightening muscles in her belly, while the muscles in her thighs went limp and loose.

That indefinable magick moved through her, throbbing and pulsating, stroking her like an invisible hand. *What is that…* She gasped as it rubbed itself over a spot buried by her womb, with hard, firm little circles, until she was rocking back against Ronal and sobbing. Against the curve of her bottom, she could feel the firm ridge of his cock and she slid her hands back, gripping his hips and bringing him more firmly against her.

Her pussy grew hot and slick as cream pooled there. Her clit started to throb as that indefinable magick roamed over her body.

A hand stroked her hair. His mouth caressed her ear and distantly, Caet heard him whisper, "You have nothing to fear from me, Caetria." The sharp scrape of his teeth against her neck, more of that magick caressing her inside.

Then his teeth slid into her neck, a quick, burning pain that exploded into fiery pleasure that shot through her veins in a shimmery rain with every beat of her heart as he fed. One big, warm hand came up and cupped her breast through her blouse, milking the nipple, abrading it with the silk of her shirt.

His other hand lay alongside her cheek, resting there as his mouth worked at her neck. A moan rumbled out of his chest as he whispered into her mind, *You taste sweet, powerful… I've not had a woman like you in…forever.*

Caet cried out as the stroking of magick deep within her womb quickened and she exploded in his arms, climaxing with a rush, wetness flowing from her in waves. Ronal pulled his mouth from her neck and growled, whirling her around and lifting her, using his hands to guide her legs around his waist. He pumped his cock against the covered, damp cleft between her thighs, shuddering as she moaned and whimpered her way through the orgasm, tears streaming from her eyes.

Caet's eyes widened as he pushed his tongue deep inside her mouth and she tried to pull away. But she could taste nothing more than him, just that intoxicating honeymead of his kiss, even though he had just finished feeding from a vein.

She rocked hungrily against his sex, one hand twining in the black silk of his hair. The other, she slid inside the cotton of his shirt. A heavy chain at his neck met her fingers and she wrapped them around it, pulling her head back and gasping for air. Wiggling her hips, she worked herself up and down against his covered cock, starving, desperate to feel his length inside her.

Ronal stared at her. Her hair fell in flaxen waves around her slim, straight shoulders, the heart-shaped perfection of her face flushed as she sucked in air and stared at him. He braced her weight with his hands under her taut little butt, his head still swimming from the pure, heady power of her blood. All that was ancient, her taste was sweet, seductive and so damned divine... He blinked as her fingers withdrew from under his shirt, sliding down to the leather of his jerkin, plucking at the lacings as she went and spreading it open.

Then she leaned back, just slightly, gripping the bottom of her shirt, pulling it over her head, the ends of her hair drifting down to cover her breasts, her nipples peeking through the thick locks at him as she slid her hands up his chest, digging her nails lightly into his flesh. She tangled her hands in his hair and leaned forward, catching his lower lip in her mouth, tugging lightly, laughing huskily when he groaned. One hand went to his shirt, tugging at the laces and pushing it open. His skin was so warm, so smooth. She wanted to feel him against her.

"Caet—"

Her lashes lifted and she raised her hand, pressing a finger to his lips. A hot, sinful smile danced in her eyes as she went back spreading his shirt open with that one hand. The other she still had buried in his hair, and she helped anchor her weight with her knees gripping him on either side at his hips.

But when she got to the laces that held his breeches closed, she had to release her hold on his hair and lean back. He balanced her a little more, shifting his grip to her waist, spreading his legs wider. He breathed shallowly, staring at her bent head, his cock jerking with each innocent brush of her fingers against his covered flesh.

Finally, she had the lacings free and she jerked them open, his cock springing out. She traced her finger up his length before staring at him, her lids lowered to half-mast, the full ivory globes of her breasts rising and falling with the unsteady motions of her breathing.

"Fuck me," he muttered. "If you aren't the most beautiful thing I've ever seen..."

Caet laughed and plucked at the waist of her breeches. "I still have the problem of my breeches," she mused.

Ronal swore and said, "Not a problem." He found the seam at her back and jerked, ripping them. "Not a problem," he repeated, his voice shaking a little now as he lifted her and started to lower her onto his cock, staring at the smooth, hairless cleft. Moisture gleamed on the swollen petals of her pussy as he spread her thighs wide, holding her open as he pushed inside.

"Hmmm, look at that—such a pretty sight," he muttered as he watched his cock stretch that plump, smooth flesh.

Her soft gasp spurred him on and he lifted his eyes, watching her face, as he took her deeper. "You're so tight," he said, his body shaking with the urge to throw her down and mount her, mark her, claim her.

Her snug little pussy convulsed around his cock, clenching and releasing in a maddening milking sensation that he was sure would rob him of his sanity.

As he stared at her, Caet's tongue slid out, tracing over the full curve of her lower lip. "Ummm," she muttered, her head falling back.

Under his hands, he felt the muscles of her taut little ass flex and he squeezed, pulling out and pushing back inside. The walls of her pussy resisted him and he gritted his teeth as he forged slowly into her. Sinking to his knees, he reached out and snagged her shirt and the leather bodice, spreading them on the forest floor before he laid her down, blanketing her body with his, draping her thighs over his as he pushed deeper inside her slick little pussy.

"Say my name," he whispered against her mouth. "I've dreamed of feeling this lovely body against me since I saw you."

"Ronal," she murmured, digging her nails into his shoulders and arching her hips up against him, whimpering in protest when he pulled out.

Then he sank back inside and she shivered, the tight buds of her nipples stabbing into his chest, her pussy clenched around his cock, and her core wept. His eyes met hers and he smiled, a wicked smile, then the magick returned and she was feeling that hot, shimmering touch inside her again.

"What is that…?"she whimpered.

"My gift," he whispered. "Payment, of sorts, for letting me feed."

Hot, molten jealousy passed through her as she thought of him sharing this with another woman. She locked her thighs around him, as though she could keep him from leaving her and going to another for anything—for feeding, for loving, for anything.

Winding her fingers in his hair, she pulled his head to hers and pressed her mouth against his, feeling the cool slick surface of his fangs against her lips, shuddering as he swiveled his pelvis and drove his cock deep inside her sheath. Whimpering, she shifted, trying to take him deeper inside. One big hand cupped the smooth curve of her bottom, stroked down her hip, down her leg to her ankle, guiding that leg around his waist, forcing her open, to take more of his impaling length.

Caet gasped, her head falling back, as she stared into his eyes. From under a fringe of lashes, he watched her. "You are the most amazing creature I've ever held in my arms," he whispered, pulling out and then shuddering as he slowly slid his length back inside her.

She could feel him inside her, thick and swollen, sliding slickly through the wet folds of her pussy, stroking deep within before he pulled his cock out and started that slow, maddening process all over again.

His lashes lowered and his head fell back, exposing the long, strong line of his neck, a groan rumbling out of his chest.

Tears stung her eyes, and her heart ached within her chest. She had never seen a more beautiful man in all her life. Burying her face against his shoulder, she sank her teeth into his chest and sobbed.

He throbbed and jerked inside her and she whimpered, clenching around him and throwing back her head, a scream rippling out of her before his head swooped down and he swallowed the sound down. His hand flexed on her ass as he moved harder and faster inside her, groaning raggedly deep within his chest, purring softly in her mind, *We'll find a place, sometime, someplace, where I can make you scream all night long. And it will be my name on your lips, pet.*

Caet sobbed out, "Yes..." and then she screamed his name against his lips as her orgasm ripped through her, her pussy clasping at his cock as the tissues rippled and clenched around him.

"That's it, pet," he crooned against her lips. "Come for me, let me feel it...such a tight, hot little pussy...come for me..."

She trembled and jerked in his arms as the orgasm ripped through her. His cock swelled within her, the thick column of flesh jerking, rasping against the slick, sensitive folds of her sheath and then he exploded inside her. Thick molten seed spewed into her as he tore his mouth from hers and bellowed her name to the skies.

Caet felt his warm presence at her back as he cuddled against her, his hand on her hip, one leg thrown over hers, his long heavy cloak of hair spread over her shoulders and chest like a silken blanket.

She hadn't ever felt so…treasured by a man after lovemaking in her life.

Lovemaking. How odd. It hadn't ever felt like lovemaking before. Not even when she had lost her virginity to the man she had thought she loved in her twenties. The young, incredibly dashing elvish healer had fascinated her, overwhelmed her…and he had definitely enjoyed fucking the king's daughter. And then once it came out that was what he had been after, he had held her in his arms and stroked her back, murmuring, "I do care for you, Caet. But we're both so young…"

She hadn't ever felt like a man had truly wanted to be with her just for the hell of being with her, she mused. Not until now.

And it wasn't with one of her own. But with a vampire.

She felt him press a kiss to the top of her head, then his breath moved her hair as he murmured, "I almost hate to ask what you are thinking, Caetria."

"Nothing, truly," she lied, sinking her teeth into her lip and staring into the forest, lit softly by the night-blooming lavender. The flower's perfume was sweet and heady and she closed her eyes, breathing it in.

Propping himself up on his elbow, he stared down into her face and laughed softly. "Liar. That canny mind of yours doesn't ever slow its thinking," he mused, reaching out and catching a blossom that was far out of her reach. Bringing it to her, he stroked the softly glowing petals up the line of her arm, over the curve of her breast, teasing her nipple with it, before tucking it behind her ear. "Your eyes are too sad for you to be thinking of nothing."

Rubbing his thumb over her lip, he asked, "Will you tell me of your mother?"

Her lashes drooped. Turning her head aside, she asked quietly, "What is to tell? She walked too often and too far into the world of power. Father begged her to cease her daily walking, but she couldn't resist the call of sorcery. Thus, she left us." Caet's eyes turned away from his as they started to burn and sting. "It still hurts so, even to think of her now. And he is calling her back, after all this time. How do we know she is not mad?"

"If she is mad, his call will not affect her. He calls only those who still hear him as their leader. Those who are lost to the madness know only the madness as their leader," Ronal murmured, stroking her arm gently. "She did what she felt she must, Caet. Know that, whatever else happens. She did what she felt she must."

"Leaving her child and her loving husband behind?" Caet said, her voice sullen. Closing her eyes, she said flatly, "In all these years, more than two centuries, he has never loved another, never taken another mate. Always he has waited for her return, and never has she come. If for no other reason, I cannot forgive the pain she has caused him."

"Perhaps it pained her as well. But have you thought that she was protecting you?" Ronal whispered.

"Protecting me?" Caet asked, her body going cold. She rolled from his arms and searched around for her clothing. Her breeches were ruined. Spying her shirt sticking out from under them, she jerked on it demandingly until he rolled enough to let her pull it free.

With quick, jerky motions, she tugged it over her head before asking, "How could she possibly hope to protect me by leaving me?"

"Her soul was lost to the call of sorcery, Caetria," Ronal said, arching his hips up and tugging his breeches back into place before he rose and laced them up. "But her heart…if she had no love for you, there was no reason why she couldn't stay. She would have no care if you and your father watched her slip farther into madness. If that indeed was where she was going. The battle with sorcery can be a terrible one, a lonely one. It takes away everything from a person. Their souls, their lives…it shouldn't cost her what precious time she may have with her daughter as well."

"She could have had two hundred years, if she had chosen to," Caet said, feeling her throat tighten. "She just didn't want them."

"You would have hated her even more if she had stayed. Sorcery isn't something you can understand, unless you have it inside you," Ronal said. "It is almost like an illness, a cancerous thing that eats away at you and calls to you every waking hour. 'Tis not a lovely sweet magick like enchantment can be, nor a heady rush like witchery, nor the wondrous thing that Healing can be. Sorcery, unless that person wielding it is very strong, can be a twisted fouled thing. And if it took her into the blackness, she wouldn't have it infecting you as well."

Caet cupped her arms around herself, staring into the night, feeling an aching cold settling into her bones. "You sound as though you know much of sorcery," she whispered.

Ronal said softly, "My mother was a sorceress. She walked away from me when I was but an infant. I saw her once, when I was…maybe ten. And then she asked my father to kill her. The darkness was crowding in on her, too fast and too strong. She wasn't as strong as some."

Caet's breath left her in a startled gasp. "Oh." She fell to her bottom, unaware that a branch from the trees bent to catch her from hitting the hard ground. She swayed in midair, staring at him with dark, bruised eyes. "Why would she ask him?"

"Because she trusted no other," Ronal said. His eyes glittered in the darkness. Turning away, he closed his eyes. "I knew nothing of this for many years. And when I learned of it, my father and I did not speak for nearly four decades. By the time I spoke with him again, I had learned more of sorcery, and how badly it can tear their minds. She was never the woman she had been when my father first met her. Sorcery changes a person. Only a bonding with a creature who was born to walk in the world of power could possibly prevent a sorceress from dying inside, a little bit every day of their lives."

Caet leaped off of her soft little swing, and the branch retreated. Her eyes snapped as she hissed, "If it is such a terrible power, then why is it given to anybody? Why would the Ancient One curse anybody so?"

Catching the hand she slammed into his chest, Ronal stared down into her angry face. Poor thing. He cupped her cheek, rubbing his thumb across her lower lip. "Sometimes, the magick we wield within us, outside of sorcery, isn't enough. Enchantment is a wonderful thing, and witches are sheer amazement. Healers are miraculous. But sometimes—you need a warrior who is even more than that."

"So a man is given a gift that will drive him mad," she said huskily. "Just to fight a battle that should never have been his in the first place. This fight that is coming our way…it isn't a battle for elves. 'Tis not us they seek. It is the Gatekeepers."

Ronal cocked a brow at her. "One of the Gatekeepers is an elf. And one of the Pillar Gates, one that could destroy the very foundation of this world if the wrong man set his will upon it, is within your boundaries." He ran his hand through the tumbled silk of her hair, watching as the curls tangled around it as through they had a life of their own. She was so lovely, so pure, so fiery. "A war is coming to pass, within Mythe. This is not a war just upon my brothers. It is a war upon our world.

"Your people long ago settled the Wood of Glynmare, and the wood is indeed part of Mythe. What would destroy Mythe, will destroy the wood." Ronal watched as her eyes narrowed.

"You do not know if that is true," she said, her voice trembling with the intensity of her anger.

He lifted his face, his lashes lowering, as he took a deep breath. "I have walked this world for more than a thousand years. It is changing, the very air around me. I feel rage, I feel anger, and I feel fear. Even the land is preparing for battle — do you not hear how silent the wood has become in the past months? Not all of the game has fled, but it is…waiting. The younger herds have moved on and some of the predators have followed. Everything waits."

Caet's heart went cold as she realized just how serious he was. And how very right he was.

Licking her lips, she pulled away from him. "If war must come to Mythe, then the elves will meet it head on. We will not cower in the wood and be picked off clan by clan," she said woodenly.

Kneeling, she grabbed her bodice and her torn trousers and then she turned and disappeared into the wood, her head bowed low.

Chapter Five

It was late the next morning when she took audience with the *Esri*. With her father, she needn't take audience. But when meeting with him as the Elf King, she needed an audience.

She hadn't slept. Not since she had left Ronal's arms. Disquiet surged within her, side by side with fear. Was the vampire right?

Were they in such danger? Not just the people, but all of Mythe?

Lowering herself to sit on the floor, she crossed her legs in front of her. Daklin studied her with worried eyes from his place at Matiro's left hand. They were the only ones in the *sekrine*. Caet folded her hands in her lap and lifted solemn eyes to her father's face. "Have you heard from any of the sorcerers, *Esri*?"

He lifted one straight blond brow at her, his cool gray eyes curious. But he answered in a bland, easy tone. "Indeed. Several were already en route to the wood, but they are traveling from afar. Some will take weeks to reach us. 'Tis strange. They felt an urging from within to come to the wood, a strong one, and some have been traveling home for months already. We shall be seeing them arrive as early as the morrow."

Her throat felt tight and dry as she swallowed. So soon. Closing her eyes, she whispered, "And the Lady Asmine?"

Matiro's eyes flickered ever so slightly. "She will be among the first to arrive." He sighed, and his hand clenched, a sign of how very anxious he was. "I am—anxious to see her, Caet. I do ask that you recall who she is."

Caet lowered her head in a nod. "The vampire spoke of things very odd last night," she said, her voice low and hushed.

Daklin's eyes narrowed on her. She could feel his measuring gaze and she kept her own eyes averted as her cousin said levelly, "He speaks of odd things often. Odder still, how often he is right."

"This time, he spoke of war."

Matiro leaned back, his eyes reflecting the light of the witchlights that danced on the walls, making reading them impossible. "War will come to Mythe," he said softly.

Caet said, "You said last night that you called the sorcerers back to protect us from death."

He smiled gently. "From useless death, love. I cannot stop a war that is already in the making," he said softly, sliding from the carved wooden chair to kneel in front of her. The father spoke to his daughter, not the king to a subject, or a king to his heir, as he said, "War will come, because evil men will always be in the world. And if we do nothing, then the evil has already won."

He closed his eyes and when he opened him, the stately mantle of a king had settled back over him and he slid back into his chair. "War will come. With war, comes death. But we are the People of the Wood and we are not unknown to battle. We will prepare and we will triumph. The sorcerers come to help rebuild our shielding, to help us prepare in whatever ways only a sorcerer can. With the shielding in place, those of our people who are not warriors can remain in relative safety until, if or when, the time comes to travel into the Mountain Realm."

"The Mountain Realm?" Caet asked. She didn't want to travel there. Her mountain kin were crazy.

Matiro smiled, his eyes twinkling as though he knew exactly what she was thinking. "Indeed, the Mountain Realm. The mountains can withstand any force known to man," he said, a grin flirting with his mouth. "So very isolated the elves of the mountains are."

"Might explain why they are so very crazed," she whispered. "Inbreeding."

Matiro muffled a laugh. "I think they do make sure they marry outside each individual clan every few generations," he said drolly. "The High King would surely see to that."

"Would you?"

"Daily," he said, rolling his eyes at his impudent daughter.

His hand reached inside his tunic, and Caet stilled as he brought out a silver chain...the seal of Caval, the one he had tried to give to Ronal. Caet had seen him toy with the seal often, knew how he valued it, although until the *Esri* had spoken with Ronal, she'd had no idea why. It had been a kind thing for Ronal to do, letting the *Esri* keep the seal. She stared at it as her father ran the chain through his fingers and paused to rub his thumb across the stone.

"Daughter mine," Matiro murmured. "Do you know, since the days of the vampire and elf wars, we finally stopped acting as a solitary unit? The people learned, once more, to fight as they had in old, as one people, instead of many. That is something we shall need in the days to come."

He sighed and tucked the chain away. Reaching for a scribe and parchment, he said, "'Tis time, though, that we gather our Clans of the Wood together. We must prepare."

"Da, if war is coming to Mythe, shouldn't we prepare to fight?" she asked softly.

Matiro's daughter was a warrior. He knew this.

But she was his only heir. Risking her to the war would be risking his people.

Closing his eyes, he waited until she had left and turned his eyes to Daklin. "What am I to do now?" he said quietly. "I cannot risk her."

Daklin lifted a brow. "And you sound as though you do not know if you can lead your warriors into war," his nephew said insightfully.

"I am old, Daklin. I am sixteen hundred years old," he said quietly. "I was old when I fathered Caetria. Asmine was a sweet, passing beauty in my life. I never thought she would get with child, but when she did, it was the most amazing thing..." his voice trailed away. "For the longest time, we prepared for the fact that you would be the heir. Do you ever regret that you will not be?"

Daklin laughed. "I have enough trouble just dealing with that blasted Gate," he said truthfully. "Caet will make an honest and true *Esrine*, one I am honored to serve. Once she grows up."

Matiro chuckled tiredly. "Indeed. Much growing she needs to do," he murmured. Then a frown crossed his face. "Although the woman who just left here wasn't the same petulant child I dealt with a few weeks ago."

Daklin wisely kept his mouth shut, although he couldn't hide the gleam in his eyes. Matiro arched a brow at him. "I haven't taken leave of my senses, lad. And I'm quite aware of what happens within my wood, especially since it took place in the *open* wood. And I do not think a quick tumble with a vampire is enough to make her mature overnight. However, being forced to face the fact that he isn't what she expected just may have opened her eyes and started her down the road."

He headed out of the main room and paused, turning to glance at Daklin over his shoulder. "Do you think that you could mention to Ronal how in touch I am with my wood? I'd rather not spend another night like last night. 'Tis bad enough when I spend night after lonely night, without my lady wife by my side," Matiro said, a grim smile on his face. "But knowing that your *daughter* is vigorously enjoying herself is rather...disturbing. Her *sekrine* keeps such connection from happening. As would any other dwelling. Or rock shelf...or water...but the land—"

Daklin had to bite the inside of his cheek to keep from laughing. Folding his face into somber lines, he bowed slightly. "Of course, *Esri*," he said softly. Then he said, "If Asmine was just a passing beauty, why did you take her to wife?"

Matiro's face closed down. "'Tis an easy thing to fall in love with somebody who gives you an amazing gift, Daklin," the Elf King said softly. "A very easy thing. And she was such a sweet, winsome creature. Once...before the sorcery laid its hold so deeply upon her."

Then he walked away, lost in his memories.

* * * * *

The Lady Asmine's arrival wasn't a celebrated affair. She simply walked into the wood, wrapped in a cloak that covered her from head to toe in filmy, glowing white.

When she pushed the hood back from her face, she stared around her with dark, haunted eyes, lashes lowering to hide her lavender irises from those who met her gaze.

Until she saw her daughter striding out from her father's *sekrine*. And then her eyes widened and tears flooded her gaze. Her lips trembled for a moment before she pressed them together and then her face firmed and she lifted her chin. Asmine planted her feet on the ground, and waited as the woman swung her way, eyes locked on her face.

It was like staring into a mirror, Asmine thought, as her daughter slowed to a stop in front of her. A much kinder mirror. Sorcery hadn't hollowed her down to sinew, bone and muscle. Nor had it placed shadows in her eyes—Matiro's gift of Enchantment had been much stronger in Caet's blood than the sorcery. Asmine thanked the Ancient Ones that Caetria would never battle the dark insanity that could take those who walked in the world of power.

That was why she had left. Walking within the world of power had pulled her too far, too fast. And her grip on reality for a time had become tenuous. By the time she had once more stabilized, nearly fifty years had passed. She had thought of coming back. But before the journey had even started, the darkness had called her again.

And Asmine knew she would never be safe from the insanity of her magick. The sorcery had frayed the edges of her mind and even though sometimes she could walk in the world and maintain her sanity for weeks or months at a time, the world of power would call her. And magick would ripple through her mind, exploding through her veins as her gift used her.

It would, in time, overtake her, unless she died first. Over the centuries the calling from the world of power had become more frequent. She couldn't stay away like she once had. And sometimes when she looked at things, she was starting to see them in both worlds.

It was getting close to the time.

No—she would never allow one she loved to see her body wither and die as her soul slid away, lost forever in a world of enchantment and magick. Death like that wasn't true death...her body was gone, but her soul went on, adding it to the world of power, and trapping her, forever. It was a terrible way to die.

And she wouldn't do it.

Asmine would seek her death in time. If her body and soul died together, instead of splitting apart, she'd go on to the Heavens, to be with her people.

After this.

Staring into Caetria's eyes, she tried to think of something to say but couldn't find a single word. Swallowing, she finally whispered, "You became a lovely woman, Caetria."

With an arrogant lift of her chin, the *Esria* said, "I had some time in which to do it. More than two hundred years."

Asmine chuckled. "You've learned temperance in those years, *vaetcha*. Is that the most cutting thing you have to say to the woman who abandoned you?" she asked gently.

So close they stood, Asmine could see Caet's throat work as she swallowed, watched as the golden-dusted tips of her black lashes flickered. "Do not call me *vaetcha*," Caet finally whispered, her voice husky and whisper soft. "You haven't the right."

Then she turned and walked away.

Asmine sighed. "You are my beloved daughter, Caet, whether you believe that or not," the Sorceress murmured.

A silken, dark voice coaxed, *Why should she believe? You walked away from her…they never once came for you. They do not love you like I…come back to me…come live in the power. Be one with us.*

Asmine shuddered as the world of power tried to summon her. *Be silent*, she commanded.

As the power whispered to her, she strode down the path that led to the central part of the High Clan's home. There, she would find her husband. And yet another heartbreak to deal with.

Ronal watched as Caet walked away from her mother.

He should have known that Asmine, Lady of the White, was her mother.

She was one of the more powerful sorcerers. And the call had laid its mark heavily on her. Almost brutally so. Her form was reed slender, her face hollow, her eyes nearly too large in her thin face.

But they were Caet's eyes, and the pure beauty of her face was Caet's. Even the sorrow he had seen in Asmine's eyes was the same as the sorrow he saw in Caet's.

Asmine was losing the battle, though. Caet wouldn't have her mother much longer. Asmine spent too much time in the world of power and her time in the world was running short. Ronal had seen that look before.

She would seek her own end soon.

"Lady Asmine," he murmured at her shoulder.

She turned and when she saw his face, a ghost of a smile flirted with her mouth. "Lord Ronal, whatever is a Gatekeeper doing so deep in the wood, and so very far from his own keep?" she asked, her voice deep and hollow.

"A common enemy has threatened us all," Ronal murmured, frowning as he remembered the explosion that had come raining down on him from out of the ceiling of his keep weeks earlier. And now, it had happened here, in the wood. "Something seeks to kill the Gatekeepers, and now the People of the Wood."

"A foolish enemy, we have," she said, her voice drifting off as her eyes closed. Her head fell back and Ronal remained silent as she absorbed the energy from the land. What it told her, he had no idea, but when her eyes opened, the lavender orbs were glowing with an insane fire. "They think to take us on our own land, the fools."

"You can see them?" he asked quietly.

"No, but I can feel their intent," she murmured. "They think the elves weak. Enchantment takes too long to build and it would take the lives of many to rebuild the walls they destroyed. They've laid a foul evil inside our land, thinking to weaken us." Her eyes flashed from lavender to purple, glowing in her rage, casting a frightening light on the shadows of her pale face.

Ronal smiled and laid a gentle hand on her shoulder. "Asmine, be calm. They weren't counting on the sorcerers."

Asmine blinked, and then she smiled. It was a haunting, deadly smile. "No. They were not."

* * * * *

"It doesn't matter that we didn't kill the Elf King and his heir," the master said to Remero later that same night. "We shall simply move in now. Their shielding is down and we've laid our mark upon the land. The shielding around the wood is millennia old. Enchanters sink their protection into it as they come of age. It would take giving up their lifeblood to reestablish protection upon it, the lives of several."

"Enchantment is a rather powerful magick," Remero said softly, stroking his cheek. "Just because it takes time to build doesn't mean we should discount it. And couldn't they get protection from other magicks?"

The master laughed. "They cast out other magicks long ago. Sorcerers are unwelcome in their own lands, and only they could have protected them, because witchery is unknown to them. It simply doesn't run in their bloodline. A line of warrior witches could present problems, but they haven't had a warrior witch born to them in millennia. The satyr, damned his horned head, has his own earth magick but he isn't enough to protect an entire wood. No, the People of the Wood shall fall to my new army."

Remero smiled. "The sorcerers are very eager to go out and play," he said, stroking his hand down his beard. "Very eager indeed. Shall I rouse them?"

"Aye. And prepare the infantry as well. I have been preparing these men for years. Now it is time," the master murmured, his rheumy old eyes lighting with an unholy fire. "Now it is time."

* * * * *

They came.

Sometimes singly. Often in small pairs or trios. Sometimes in groups of ten or twenty. Once an entire group of solemn, unsmiling elves, their numbers in the hundreds. By the time a week had passed, more than a thousand sorcerers had returned to the wood and set up an encampment outside the main clan home.

Messengers had come winging in from outlying clans, and Caet watched with grim eyes as a fire-haired elf arrived from the People of the Mountains.

With her arms crossed, and her heart heavy, she stood silently at her father's side as he read the missive from the People of the Mountains.

We hear whispers of War coming our way. I have sent two bands of my most elite warriors. My people retreat farther into the Mountains and you are welcome to join us. The People of the Wood are welcome to all that we have in times of peace and of trouble.

Konar

Below his signature was the seal of the Elf King of the Mountain People. "Does the *Giani* really think retreat into depths of the mountains is necessary now?" Caet asked softly, watching as her mother led a small group of sorcerers into the heart of the clan.

Her mother's hair had gone silver.

It had once been the same pale blonde as Caet's, shot through with strands of darker blonde, mingled with strands of every shade of gold imaginable.

But it was silver now, almost the sparkling color of *diame*. There should have been a coronet of the precious metal at Lady Asmine's brow, but she had walked away from it years ago.

Oh, she was still lovely...and if one could look at her without truly seeing her eyes, those dark, troubled eyes, Asmine looked ageless, much like Matiro did. But then, looking into her eyes—

"You look so bitter, child," Matiro said, a quiet sigh escaping him as he handed the missive to Daklin. "Your mother did what she felt she must. The years have not been...kind to her."

"How do you know?" Caet asked harshly. She could only think of how often she had looked at him and seen the loneliness haunting his eyes. How often she had needed her mother, and the woman hadn't been there. Yet her father spoke as though he expected her to forgive her mother, as though he already had. "She walked away so long ago, and never once came back. How can you possibly know?"

"I have only to look," Matiro whispered. "The woman I knew was full of laughter. The sorcery has stolen that from her."

Daklin moved between Asmine and the *Esri* and *Esria* before Caet could speak, bowing low. "Lady Asmine, Lady of the White. Ronal has spoken often of the Lady of the White, and how powerful her sorcery is, how great her heart," Daklin murmured, catching her hand and lifting it to his lips. "Had I known it was my own aunt..."

Asmine chuckled, the sound rough, as though she hadn't laughed in ages. She tugged her hand away and said, "You've been charming people since before I was born, Daklin, Gatekeeper of the Wood." Although she was the younger by two centuries, when she lifted her eyes, she looked ancient. She stepped across the boundary and entered the formal grounds that made up the *Esri*'s outdoor court. Halfway across it, she dropped to one knee and curtsied low.

"*Esri, en kiane fiun suare,*" Asmine murmured, keeping her eyes low.

The sorcerers behind her kept their eyes averted, although Caet could see surprise in some. How many had realized the woman they had appointed unofficial leader was wife to the Elf King?

Caet was too busy trying to translate the archaic elvish to watch her father. It wasn't until she felt the sigh leave his body that she realized how tense he was. His hands were clenched into fists, although they rested in his lap, so none would be likely to see it. His shoulders were rigid and his eyes were locked on Asmine's lowered head.

Caet started to reach out to touch his shoulder, but he leaned forward, his eyes softening as he stared at his wife. "Asmine, *michan*, do not bow before me. Not my wife," he whispered in a soft, low voice that just barely carried to her ears.

In an equally quiet voice, Asmine replied, "I no longer have the right, or the honor, to call myself that."

Matiro arched a brow. "But I still wish to call you that. Are you denying me that pleasure?" he asked.

Caet felt eyes on her, as she moved her gaze away from her parents. This wasn't something they needed to watch. This was too intimate, too private. She ignored the looks as she caught the eyes of her father's people and started to silently clear the court as best as she could. It wasn't until she was moving toward the edge of the clearing that she realized Daklin, Ronal and Cray were doing the same.

Caet hesitated briefly by her mother's side, a thousand unspoken words on her tongue, but then she just moved on, a sigh slipping past her lips as she moved on to the sorcerers. Staring into those eyes, all of them so aged and empty, she felt cold. What did the sorcery do to them?

Before she even opened her mouth, the sorcerers turned on their heels and left the clearing, walking away from the *Esri* and Asmine without speaking a word. Caet followed in their wake, feeling the three Gatekeepers at her heels. "Where is the mortal and Arys?" she asked, silence reigning behind them. "I never see them about."

"They are newly mated. They spend as much of their time…mating…as possible," Cray said, a ghost of a smile dancing on his mouth as they walked down the path away from Matiro and his lady. As they walked, the vines and leaves and branches lowered and locked behind them, enfolding the king and the Lady Asmine in total privacy.

Caet cast a silent look behind her, as a wall of green hid her father from view. "So the mortal is not staying as far away from me as she can?"

"Of course she is," Daklin replied. "You treated her so…nicely, how can you blame her?"

Caet sneered at him. "Time away from the wood has not improved your manners any, Daklin." Ronal walked silently at her left shoulder and she could feel his eyes on her, a warm, silent caress.

"Nor has your time in the wood matured you any," her cousin drawled. He paused, sliding her a measuring look. "But I must say that was amazing thoughtfulness you showed, giving your parents time alone. I wouldn't have thought it of you."

Ronal said softly, "Daklin, that mouth of yours has gotten you in trouble more than once. Rather odd you choose now to speak of wisdom."

Daklin tossed him a sour look. Then he caught sight of a slim form that drifted between the trees just to the right of them. Black hair, shot through with thick streaks of red, sleek, and moving like a mountain cat. "Hmmm... who is that?"

"Konar's emissary," Caet said softly. "Her name is Miryam. She served as Konar's personal bodyguard for a time. She's deadly. Leave her be." But she was speaking to empty air. Daklin left the moment he heard her name.

Turning her eyes to Ronal and Cray, she shrugged. "It will be his throat that gets slit in the end, I suppose."

Cray chuckled. "He is a big boy, milady," the winged one murmured, resting a hand briefly on her shoulder. "Trouble yourself none over it."

Her belly chose that moment to rumble. "I'd rather trouble myself over putting food in my belly anyway," she said, smirking as she pictured Miryam planting Daklin on his butt a time or two.

* * * * *

Ronal sipped at his wine at Caet polished off a plate of roasted treehen, wild greens, forest potatoes and some wild strawberries that looked very delectable. He imagined they'd taste rather sweet on her lips... He heard

Cray's husky chuckle and looked up to see him watching, with a grin on his face.

Am I so transparent?

As clear as glass, my friend, the fallen one murmured, shaking his dark head. He sighed, studying Caet through his lashes. *Is she as sweet as she looks?*

Ronal laughed. *Sweeter.*

Lucky bastard. Cray's wings rustled as he shifted onto his side on the backless couch, turning his head to stare out the window. The sun streamed warm and golden through the glass and Ronal watched as Cray lifted his hand, as if hypnotized, to the beam of light, letting it fall across his skin. Something dark, and lost, moved through Cray's stormy eyes, and then the fallen one moved away from the window. Before Ronal or Caet had even blinked, he was at the door of the *sekrine*, and started running, taking three long loping steps before flinging himself into the sky.

Hard, powerful beats of his wings took him aloft as Ronal moved to the door, watching as Cray went chasing after his demons yet again.

"Why is he so sad?" Caet asked quietly.

"Something was lost to him," Ronal murmured, closing his eyes as he leaned against the frame of the open doorway. The elves used no doors, nothing to close the other out. Some used a heavy fringe of glass beads or bells. Caet had roped the bells that covered her entrance out of the way when they had entered. They still clinked together musically in the breeze. "Long ago, it was lost. His heart will never be healed."

Caet rested her hand on Ronal's shoulder, the sweet scent of her body rising to taunt him as she moved closer.

"Never is such a very long time, Ronal," she whispered. "Many things can change in the span of the ages. His heart could be healed."

Ronal lifted a brow at her, shaking his head. "Nothing has healed him in all this time. Hundreds of years have not healed him."

"Years? Of course not. It will take more than time. It will take giving back what was lost," Caet said, leaning against Ronal, wrapping her arm around his waist. "All things can be returned, sometimes in another form. But all things can be returned."

Ronal rubbed his cheek against the satin softness of her hair. "I failed to realize you were such an optimistic thing, Caetria," he whispered, shifting around and pulling her up against him. His cock started to swell within the confines of his breeches and he watched as her eyes widened when she felt him start to pulse against her belly.

She smiled sleepily at him. "I can be very optimistic...under the right circumstances," she said, lowering her lashes as she rose up on her toes and swiped her tongue across his lower lip. "Like now—I am quite certain that you and I could have a very fine time in my bed. Just as fine a time as we did under the stars."

Ronal's brows rose as his temperature climbed. Bold little thing, he thought as she slid one hand down and cupped his cock through his clothing as they stood right in the doorway of her house, where any and all could see. "Ahhh...you are not a shy woman, Caetria, are you?" he asked, his voce dropping roughly.

She laughed. "Not at all," she whispered, catching his lip between her teeth and tugging. She giggled as his hands caught her around the waist and he threw her over his shoulder.

"Shy or not, I care not to fuck your sweet little body where all can see," Ronal announced before she could start freeing his cock from his trousers.

"Well, I did mention the bed," she murmured.

Caet rather liked the view, if not the angle. He had one very fine backside. Tight, firm and rounded just so. If he had let her slide just a little lower, she could have sunk her teeth into his nicely shaped ass—*oh, my*…his fingers were caressing her backside now as he carried her through the *sekrine*, into the bedchamber.

But before she could appreciate the warmth of his hand on her ass, he flung her down onto her bed and she was left staring up at him with her hair in her face. Blowing a strand out of her mouth, she watched as he sank to his knees and pulled her to the edge of the bed, tugging her to her feet and reaching for her boots, drawing first one hard-soled boot away, then the other. Then her breeches, so she was naked from the waist down.

He leaned forward, pressed his mouth to the naked folds of her sex, drawing his tongue up the bare slit and groaning. "You're wet already," he murmured against her.

Caet blushed and whispered, "I've been like this from the first time I saw you." She squirmed as he pushed her thighs apart and stared at her. "Not that I would have admitted it."

"No hair," he whispered, petting the smooth flesh.

"Few of the people have any," she said quietly, shivering as one rough finger trailed between the plump, glistening folds. Then a whimper escaped her as he slipped his finger inside his mouth, licking the cream off with a smile. "I never have. Some women do and they magick it away, but...I...oh, do that again," she demanded when he leaned forward and swirled his tongue around her clit.

He chuckled and complied, reaching behind her and supporting her weight by cupping her bottom, holding her against him and suckling on her clit with firm, insistent draws of his mouth.

"Sweet, sweet," he crooned after he pulled away and eased her down to his lap, reaching for the lacings of her vest, tugging the leather away and drawing it over her head. Then the silk shirt, tossing it to the floor, the jewel-toned throws that covered it chasing away the cool of the morning. Ronal rose, keeping his hands under her hips, pressing his mouth to Caet's belly as he spun around in a circle, grinning as she laughed, startled.

Her head was spinning when he laid her down on the velvet spread. His black hair fell around her like a silken cloak and his eyes were so intent on her face, she felt like the focus of his entire world. One hand slid down her body from her neck to her knee, gliding over every last inch, pinching her nipple, kneading the firm, rounded flesh of her breast, measuring the dip of her waist, his fingers cupping her ass and lifting her against him. He worked his cock against her cleft before sliding down to her knee and opening her to him.

Caet sobbed as the touch of his fingers came back to her breast and jolted her clear down to her toes. Her belly clenched and her breath caught in her lungs as his hand moved farther south, massaging the globe of her breast, her belly, cupping her butt...oh, if he touched her pussy, she'd have a heart storm.

But he simply moved around it.

Every last inch of her belly was pitching from the feel of his hand on her body. Damn it, just the light, firm pleasure of his touch, so easy, so sure… It was enough to drive her mad. His hands slid away as he lifted up, and she wanted to scream at him to keep touching her. Pushing to his knees, he gripped the vee'd edge of his cotton shirt and tore it apart, while Caet stared up at him, her belly jittering.

"Please," she whimpered, reaching up to him as he brushed the shreds of his shirt away, reaching for his trousers.

As he untied them, he smiled gently. "Please what?" he asked softly.

Her lips parted and she licked them, staring as he untied the laces. *Oh, man…*the ruddy head of his cock peeked out at her as he worked the laces free farther down. "I want…ummm," she stammered. "You…"

"You want what, love?" he asked, freeing the last of the laces and moving back off the bed. The boots he wore were shorter than hers, and softer soled, easier to remove. They fell to the floor with a muffled thud and she watched as he shucked his trousers and stood before her, gloriously nude, his cock jerking under her wide, hungry gaze.

"What do you want, sweet?" Ronal asked, his eyes watching her closely. Like an observant, waiting wolf.

She did want something…Caet vaguely remembered…oh, yes. His hands. She had wanted him to touch her. Reaching out, she closed her hands over his cock and whispered, "I want you to touch me."

Ronal cupped her breast in his hand, flicking his thumb over her nipple. "Here?" he teased.

Lowering her head, she slid her tongue around the throbbing head of his cock. "No…" A salty drop of fluid seeped out and she caught it, sucking it away and humming when he bucked against her mouth.

He knelt and slid his hand up her thigh, squeezing. "How about here?" he teased.

"No—but closer," she said, shifting off of the bed and onto her knees, kneeling in front of him. The padded throws felt soft beneath her as she bent over and took him inside her mouth. He slid his hand over her rump, caressing the line between the cheeks of her bottom as he moved closer to her pussy.

Ronal stared down at her, watching as she started to move her head up and down, taking his cock in and out of her mouth, making his cock gleam wetly. He groaned and Caet could feel the vibrations shuddering through his cock.

"This is a picture I shall keep with me for ages," Ronal muttered, his other hand moving to catch the heavy curtain of her hair, pushing it aside.

Caet could feel his eyes on her and she trembled, feeling her nipples tighten even more. Her nerve endings started to sing as he slid his hand down her back, his fingers stroking the line of her spine as he shifted around, moving so that she knelt more to the side.

Craning her neck around, she continued to suckle on the thick, rigid flesh of his cock while he moved his hand over her bottom as he started to stroke her ass, his hips moving with short, hard circles against her mouth. His breathing was harsh, rough as she felt his hands grip her head. "Enough," he growled.

Caet hummed in her throat, reaching for him, but he had his hands on her hips, turning her, gripping her hands and laying them on the bed. He shoved his knee between her thighs, spreading them wide, a harsh growl trickling from his lips. Jerking her back against him, she felt the thick, hard length of him against her ass before he palmed his cock and repositioned, driving deep, burying half his length inside her with one thrust before pulling out.

Reaching back, Caet tried to catch his hips, but he caught her hands, lacing his fingers with hers and holding them flat to the bed. "I want to fuck you," he growled, holding still…waiting it seemed. He was half within her sheath and his cock swelled, throbbing, her sensitized flesh clenching around him.

Caet whimpered, catching her breath as his words sucked the air right out of her. But she forced herself to think. She understood, she thought, what he wanted. He wanted *this*, just this and nothing from her but acceptance. He wanted to take…a hot spasm tore through her and she sobbed, "Yes," as her hands clutched at his.

Ronal growled, pulling out and driving back inside her with bone-jarring force, his sex cleaving through the wet tissues of her pussy. She screamed as he seated himself inside, pulled out, and then slammed back into her, over and over. His cock swelled and she sobbed, her head falling forward onto the bed, her hair spilling around her. Ronal bent over her, scraping the exposed line of her neck with his teeth and laughing when she shuddered.

The air was heavy with the scent of their mingled sweat, her cream. Dragging in a breath of it made her belly clench, inflaming her. The sounds—his harsh, heavy breathing, his cock sliding wetly in and out of her—the scents, the feel of his sex deep inside her pussy, made her wail under the onslaught to her senses.

Her womb convulsed and she trembled, the climax building inside her belly, expanding, forcing the air out of her lungs, her eyes going dark with the force of it.

Her spine arched, her eyes closed, and still he pumped inside her, the stroke that would let her come just not...coming. He reached under her, spread open the folds that hid her clit and stroked his finger back and forth over it, gently, lightly. She hissed and tried to rub herself harder against him but he bore his weight forcefully onto her and just wouldn't let her.

"I'm fucking you," he growled. "I choose when you come."

Caet turned her head and sank her teeth into his arm and he stilled for a brief second, then he pulled out. Pushed in. Hard. Again. And again. And again, while his finger circled with slow, maddening strokes over her clit, designed to keep her from coming.

"I am fucking you," he repeated. "You gave me this..." he reminded her. "Do you want to come?"

Caet sobbed as she tried to move again, circling her hips, but he only moved away and slowed his strokes even more.

"Do...you...want...to...come?"

"Yes!" she screamed.

And just like that, he scraped his thumb over her clit and started to shaft her with deep short drives of his hips, his cock passing over that one little spot in her pussy and she started to scream, her eyes opening wide as the orgasm tore through her. Her nails bit into the hand that was still laced with hers, her pussy clenching around his cock.

His back arched and he drove into her one final time, his hoarse shout echoing off the walls as he started to come, the hot splash pooling deep inside her.

His cock jerked rhythmically as he came, pumping his hips against the curve of her ass—softer, slower strokes now—his hands caressing her hips, his voice a wordless, soft purr that wrapped a fist around her heart and squeezed.

Then he bent down and kissed her between her shoulder blades. "You are really starting to disturb me, Caetria," he whispered.

Her eyes started to sting.

Damn it. She could say the same to him.

Chapter Six

Ronal let the *kekri* buck slip to the ground, his body jerking slightly. His throat spasmed at the flat, metallic taste of the blood he swallowed. It was what he needed to fill the empty hollow inside him, but it wasn't particularly pleasant.

And his soul hungered for more. He hungered for Caetria. He checked the lifesource of the buck and found the creature was drifting in sleep, dreaming, chasing after a young doe whose scent enticed him.

Rising, he let his head fall back as the rush of energy ran through his body. Feeding always hit him with a furious passion, flooding his veins, his belly, his heart, his very being with a near violent force. Heat shuddered through his veins as he turned away from the buck and headed back to the clan, the glow of hunger fading from his eyes.

Though the fury of hunger had faded, his body ached.

He wanted to sink his aching sex inside Caet's sweet pussy, and feel her soft body against his while she slept. Listen to her heartbeat. He didn't sleep as much as she did. The more he fed, the less rest he needed. Since he had fed from her and the *kekri* buck, it would be a while before he needed much sleep. But he wanted to feel her against him.

She was getting to him. Too quickly. And too intensely. This wasn't good, he thought as his feet started to move swiftly over the forest trail. Faster and faster until the trees blurred by him as he ran. He could smell her, even though miles separated them. Her scent haunted him already, lingered when she wasn't with him. His heart jerked as he thought of leaving the wood without her when the time came.

But the time would come and he would leave.

There was no choice.

He had to be with his Gate. He was tied to it.

And she was the heir. She would one day lead these people.

* * * * *

"Our daughter became such a lovely woman," Asmine murmured, circling around the room, not meeting Matiro's eyes. She had followed him to the *sekrine* and accepted a pewter goblet of honeymead, her eyes closing in bliss as she drank something she hadn't had in decades. "So wise, even more intelligent and generous, kinder than I had ever believed she could be. She will make a wonderful *Esrine*."

"Hmmm…'tis a good thing you didn't see her a few weeks ago. Much growing has she done in recent days." Matiro lifted a brow as Asmine continued to circle nervously, rubbing one hand against the other. Softly, he added, "Her heart isn't in it. She will lead them wisely, and well. But it isn't what she wants."

Asmine lifted startled eyes to Matiro, her hands stilling their ceaseless motions to fall slackly to her sides. "She does not want to lead the People of the Wood?"

"Her heart has never been that of a leader," Matiro murmured, his eyes moving away. They moved to the open door, following a path where his daughter had walked. "She does not want the fate of many resting in her quite capable hands. She does not want to be the one they look to—she wants her solitude, her privacy. And her freedom. The *Esri* is many things, but never free."

Asmine whispered, "I have had freedom. It is also known as loneliness."

Matiro laughed. "You left because you felt you had to. Caet has never felt she had a choice to even consider it," he said, lifting one shoulder. "It would make all the difference in the world, to one who has never had the choice."

"But she would still be alone in the world. Away from clan, from hearth and home, away from everything that is home." There were two hundred years of heartbreak in her voice as she spoke, all her aching loneliness, all her pain.

"If ever she did leave, she could still return—she wouldn't be kept away." He watched as her body jerked when he whispered into her ear. The scent of her body struck him like a fist in the solar plexus, voltar lilies and silkwater. "You could have returned at any time...I kept waiting, wishing you would."

A soft whispery breath escaped her as he drew her body back against him. The force of her sorcery arced out of her body and swept through him, heating his veins in a way he hadn't known in centuries. "You could not possibly have been waiting for me all this time," Asmine said starkly. "The woman you married died long ago."

"No. She is you, left shattered by a burden you wouldn't let me bear with you," Matiro said, fighting to keep the bitterness out of his voice. "But she is not dead. I can feel her heart—I knew the moment you returned to my wood, to me." Holding her firmly against him, he slid one hand around to cup her face and arched her back, craning his neck so that their lips met. "You've come back to me—in your heart, you know that."

Asmine shuddered under his hands as he breeched the barrier of her lips and her slender, seemingly frail form leaned into his, turning in his arms. *Yes*...she sighed longingly into his mind. *For a time.*

But the touch of her mind on his caused the flimsy barrier between their minds to collapse. The visions that had plagued Matiro for years coalesced and Asmine jerked back, her eyes widening, tears making them gleam like jewels. "*No!*" she hissed, pressing one hand to her belly, her face twisting in a furious snarl. "*No.*"

"What is meant to be," he murmured, moving to her, shaking his head. "Will be, *bechen.*" Beloved...his only beloved. She had always been the only one for him—he had waited more than a thousand years to find her, and she had spent only a handful of years with him. But it changed nothing. She was his beloved. "It is meant to happen—the visions have changed from me dying alone, holding steady the magicks that protect the people. But they only changed when you came. I went from dying alone...to dying with you at my side."

Asmine pressed her hands to her brow, shaking her head. His voice...it had haunted her so, for years and years. The warmth of his touch had heated her flesh in her dreams and when she woke, it left her achingly cold when she realized she was truly, completely alone.

And now—she had shared the vision that he would die.

Oh, she may die as well, but she had always intended to seek that end soon. Might as well die protecting the homeland she had forsaken so long ago. She had always loved it. The wood had always been in her heart.

But him? Matiro's wonderful body lying limp beside her as the magick burnt the life out of him?

"*No.*" The words left her in a ferocious snarl and she whirled, lifting her face and shrieking her denial to the sky. Startled, birds flew from the trees, and the soft hum of the forest fell into complete silence as the animals that remained went deathly still in their fear. "I will *not* allow this, Matiro."

When she turned and stared at him, he was watching her calmly, his hands linked behind his back, the dark silver of his loose tunic gleaming dully in the dim light. His blond hair, thick and straight, hung down to his hips, a simple band of *diame* at his brow, and his strong face was as handsome now as the day she had first seen him. "You cannot stop it, Asmine," he whispered, his gray eyes gentle on her face. He took a step, and then another, carefully, as though he knew how close she was to breaking. When she held her place, he reached out, and Asmine gasped as he cupped her face again, with just one hand, lifting it to his. "So lovely, you've always been so lovely," he told her. "You have become so fragile looking, like a harsh wind could knock you from the trees. My wife, my woman...my lover. Heart of my heart."

Asmine felt a hot tear burn its way down her cheek as she stared up at Matiro. "You are *Esri*, Matiro." Her voice trembled and she swallowed past the lump in her throat. "The People of the Wood need you—our daughter needs you."

"I will do what our people need. I have always done as my forefathers have whispered I must," he said, closing his eyes and lifting his face to the sky.

Wise, patient bastard, she thought. He had always been thus...believing that his steps were dictated by the Ancient God and by his forefathers. But to go willingly to his death? "Matiro—"

His fingers came up and pressed against her lips. "I've traveled, in my dreams, down the paths our people will take if I turn away from what must come, Asmine. Will you see our people falter? See the wood fall? Our protections have been breeched." He moved his hands away from her mouth and Asmine shuddered as her lips were left buzzing from his touch. His hands now threaded through her hair and unconsciously, she arched into his touch. Her heart pounded inside her chest, slow and rhythmically, as her head started to spin. "The sorcerers will rebuild it...but not here. Something in the land is tainted now, broken."

Asmine quivered when she felt his body against hers. She had moved even closer, without realizing it, until she was leaning against him, her fingers curling into the hard ridge of muscle at his neck as he spoke. Finally, through the fog of need and hunger, his words penetrated and she lifted her lashes. "We are in danger here, are we not?"

Matiro sighed against her forehead, his lips moving as he pressed a line of butterfly kisses against her skin. "Yes. We have been in danger since the protective barriers fell. The enemy will think to move against us, if he hasn't already. It is time for the People of the Wood to move deeper into our realm, away from these lands."

Grave words...so why wasn't she more frightened? Asmine knew the answer to that. It had to do with the fact that his hands were sliding down her neck, one curving around, arching her face up his, while the other hand smoothed down the unadorned front of her long robe, his fingers circling around her nipple before he cupped her breast, milking the nipple with slow, skillful strokes of finger and thumb.

She felt each touch in the pit of her belly, heat flooding her sex. Against her belly, she felt the throb of his cock under his trousers. Whimpering, she rocked against him, crushing her breasts against the hard wall of his chest. A gasp escaped her lips as her control slipped, raw magick sliding out of her grasp and flooding them both.

Matiro tore his mouth from hers, his chest heaving with his labored breathing. "Asmine, my heart…you have come back to me…not just because I called. Haven't you?" he murmured, pressing his lips to her throat.

Asmine shuddered under the hot caress of his mouth. Her heart had been pulling her back here. She had started wandering down the path that would lead her back home years ago, and with purpose for weeks. With one purpose…to see his face, to see Caetria, one last time. Urgency had filled her, knowledge that there was something she must do, and she had to see them one last time. "Yes, Matiro." Catching his face in her hands, she pressed her mouth to his, seeking out that wild, unique taste that was solely Matiro. *I came for the need to see you…be with you…*

The ground was swept out from under her feet as he caught her in his arms. Asmine pressed her face against his shoulder as he carried her down the hall.

"You will not walk away from me again," he rasped against her ear. "If you should try—I will come after you this time."

Chapter Seven

Daklin and Caetria stood shoulder to shoulder as Matiro made the announcement the following morning. Caet's eyes slid slowly between her parents, and she sighed, feeling something stir between them that hadn't been there before.

Or perhaps it had. It had simply been dormant when she had been in their company yesterday. It had, after all, been more than two hundred years since she had seen her mother. She had been little more than a child.

She forced herself to swallow past the knot in her throat, a hot, sour ball of fear building in her belly. "Da," she murmured, moving away from Daklin, taking the right that was hers as *Esria*, hers as his daughter, and kneeling before him, holding his eyes. "Is this truly needed? I seek not to question you—I trust you completely, but our homes, our lands…"

Matiro smiled, cupping her chin in his hand. "*Vaetcha*, we seek safety in the Mountain Realm, or risk dying here," he said, lowering his voice. All eyes moved away, save for Daklin and Asmine's, affording them the illusion of privacy as he brushed her hair away from her face. "It will not be forever."

Daklin took a half-step forward, dropping to one knee, and simply waited. When Matiro lifted his eyes, the Gatekeeper folded his hands across his knee and said quietly, "There is the Gate."

"What of the Gate?" Matiro asked, frowning. He tugged lightly on Caet's shoulder and she settled on her bottom at his knees, curling her arms around her legs and pinning her eyes on her cousin. She wanted to hear this as well. Beyond Daklin stood his companions, Cray on the lowest hanging limb of the tree, Arys and Pepper waiting together beneath him, their hands linked.

"The Gate's energies cannot be tainted the way our land has been," Daklin said firmly. He chose at that moment to rise and he faced the Elf King as equal, folding his arms over his chest, the small dagger sheathed to his biceps winking in the dappled sunlight. "The very nature of the Gate keeps it from happening. That is why this unknown enemy wants to be here—he thinks to be here will give him control over the land, and control over the land to him means control over the Gate. But I must first die before the Gate will submit to another. And the battle of trying to subvert a Gate, to use it for dark reasons could even kill our enemy. It would be wiser to remain, protect the Gate, our land…and stand our ground."

"If you must die," Matiro said, his eyes narrowing, a frost forming in them, "then *you* should be protected, taken to the Mountain Realm and kept safe until we discover this enemy and kill him."

Daklin shook his head. "I cannot stay so long from my Gate. Ronal and Cray are older, stronger than I, and even their magicks are not as bound to the land beneath my feet as I am. Arys draws strength from the earth itself, wherever he may be. But I need the power of home and heart, at least for a time. Enchantment binds me to my land, and to my Gate, and for me to be at my strongest, this is where I must be."

Her lips pressed together as she slid a look over her shoulder at her father, and as she suspected his eyes were gleaming, hot and furious. Lifting a brow at him, she thought about how many times he had taught her to caution her tongue, her thoughts, her features. But this was not just his people being threatened, this was his family, his blood. "Daklin, what if I tell you to that was not a suggestion, but a command from your High King?" he asked silkily, a soft, subtle threat laced in his words.

The Gatekeeper lowered his head, but revealed his hand, marked with the scar that he had carried since he had been chosen as the Gatekeeper more than five centuries ago. "I answer to no other before you, my King...save my duties to my Lord...and my duties to protect my Gate. If the Gate falls, the wood will fall."

Caet touched her fingers lightly to her father's hand. "Daklin has guarded us well, for as long as he has served as the Guardian of the Gate. Never has any evil succeeded in touching it, or in coming out of it, *Esri*," she said quietly. "He knows his duty."

Matiro arched a brow at her. Then he nodded quietly. "The land around the Gate—how many people would it hold?"

"This clan easily, more than two thousand," Daklin said calmly, without blinking an eye. "You can send other clans to the mountain realm, the smaller ones, less populated with warriors and enchanters. Those who may not be as ready to fight. But I know the High Crown Clans will stay and settle around the Gate—protect it, and the king."

The High Crown Clans, the three seed clans from which all other clans had sprung. Clan *Esriat*, the Clan of the High King, Clan *Kiarn*, Clan of the Fire Enchanters, and Clan *Feil*, the Clan of the Moonhealers. The most powerful of the clans and the ones in which the healers, the warriors and the enchanters seemed to thrive, in every generation.

"Never have we gathered the Crown Clans together," Matiro whispered, his lashes lowering, hooding his gaze.

Asmine said softly, "Times of great need call for great action. A power unlike anything the world has ever seen would be amassed, if you gathered the Crown together." She remained standing behind him, and to the side, still apart from Caetria and Matiro, but her eyes seemed less...haunted, than they had before. "*Micha*, even in Konar's mountains we may not find the safety you want for the people, if war comes."

Caet closed her eyes for a brief second. Behind her, she knew without even looking, her father was holding out his hand for his wife, and Caet's sharp ears heard her mother's nearly soundless approach. *Together, once more — but for how long this time?* she wondered, unable to stop the bitterness from welling within her.

"Caet?"

Rising, she turned her head and stared at her father, waiting. Her mother stood at his shoulder now, one hand resting there, but her eyes were watching Caet and she suspected that one sharp look from her would have the Lady Asmine withdrawing.

"*Da*, I do as you command, always. But I've been to the lands where the Gate is. From there, I believe we could fight from a position of power, instead of one of retreat," she said solemnly. "This is our land, we draw strength from it. Even though the *Giani* Konar offers us respite should we need it, I do not think we need it yet. Not Clan

Esriat." She moved her eyes restlessly around the circle, from Daklin to Cray to Arys and his mate, lingering for a long while on Ronal's face, then to her people, long, powerful and leanly built men and women, who walked in the trees like cats, who breathed magick the same way others breathed air. "We are warriors. We *fight* wars; we do not flee from them."

* * * * *

Retreating away from the talk of planning, Caet moved into the wood, finding an alcove where she could brood and worry.

Alone. Away from prying eyes, away from concerned friends…just alone.

"Well said," a deep rumbling purr of a voice sounded behind her. Unwittingly, her nipples tightened and heat splashed into her belly as she recognized that voice.

Maybe not so alone, she groused.

Konar. Damn it, not now. Ronal was drawing near, she could sense him, and she suspected finding her with an old lover would not bode well for keeping him as her present lover. Of course, she could just be reading too much into it.

"I did not realize you had followed your emissary," she said coolly, sliding out from under the hands that came up to rest on her shoulders, attempting to draw her against him.

The High King of the Mountain Realm smiled wolfishly at her. "Did you truly think I would trust the word of another when it came to this? That I'd go blindly into the Mountains without knowing if my cousins were safe? If *you* were safe," he said suggestively, stalking closer as she leaned back against a tree in an attempt to pull herself out of the sensual cloud that surrounded him. Konar drew women in, had always done so, including her. Hell, he had been one of her first lovers, and the only one she still welcomed into her bed.

Well, until Ronal. Until the vampire had laid his hands on her—but any other man after this would leave her feeling achingly empty inside. "We are fine—took an attack several weeks ago, but we withstood. With the help of a mortal witch who hates my guts," Caet said wryly, rolling her eyes as she casually moved away from him.

"But you are such a charming, winsome thing," Konar teased, catching the tail end of her braid as she tried to pass by him, using it to tug her against him. "How could anybody dislike my sweet Caet?"

"Probably because I suggested she was all but useless in aiding us." Caet pushed her hands against Konar's chest, even though the warmth of his body beckoned to her and a hundred nights shared with him rose to tease her.

"You do not seem very pleased to see me," he mused, interrupting her. Lowering his head, he breathed in the scent of her flesh along the line of her neck and then he lifted his head, his amber eyes narrowing, one black brow rising. "You've taken a lover. He is not one of us."

Caet stilled in his embrace and met his eyes. "No, he is not of fae blood. Let me go." He continued to stare at her, a tiny smile dancing on his chiseled mouth. He was so handsome...night to her day, with black hair that he wore restrained in a long braid that ended just above his very nicely muscled ass, golden skin, a body more bulky than that of the People of Wood, more adept for living and fighting in the Mountain Realm. And those eyes, the color of molten amber, warm and invasive, seeing straight through to her heart. It was no wonder her body felt the call of his.

But her heart was feeling the call of another, and her body wanted him even more.

Konar's hands slid down from her waist, gripping her bottom and lifting her, as he slowly started to rock against her cleft, his eyes still intent on hers. "Does he make you feel the way I have?" Konar whispered, lowering his head to press a kiss on the flesh bared by the loose vee of her lace-up shirt. Her nipples tightened as he breathed a puff of air along her skin and her cleft started to ache.

"No."

Ronal stood in the shadows, his arms crossed, his eyes flashing with rage, his fangs dropped. The elf holding Caet in his arms was now lifting her, palming that firm little ass, and Ronal could catch the scent of her arousal on the air.

His ears pricked as he heard the elf murmur a question to Caet. And Caet's answer shattered him.

No.

Clenching his jaw, he lifted his face to the skies and gathered his wits about him. He'd be damned if he'd storm over there since his touch meant less to her than that bastard's.

But then Caet pressed harder against the elf's chest, and she said in a strong, firm voice, "He makes me feel *more*, Konar. You come to my bed, and you share your body with me, and make me share all with you. But you don't share anything with me, you hold yourself apart from all." She arched a brow and said softly, "'Tis like having an overlarge, very talented doll in bed with me at times."

Ronal stifled a smile as the elf lowered her back to the ground, his eyes blank in the stillness of his face. "A doll, am I, Princess?" he purred.

Ronal heard the suppressed rage far better than Caet did. She apparently didn't realize, little fool, that she was messing with fire. "Hmmm, maybe not, Konar. At least a doll would still be there in the morn, wouldn't be afraid to let anybody know it was in bed with me half of the night."

Konar...bleeding hell. She was tugging the tail of the King of the Mountain Realm. Worse, she had been fucking him. Did that entail anything? Didn't matter...Ronal decided as he strode out of the shadow of the trees, his hands clenched into loose fists as he made enough racket to rouse a corpse. "Are you seeking child's things to sleep with at night, Caet?" he whispered as she whirled to face him, her eyes wide.

He pulled her against him, resisting the urge to put a brand on her. She wanted *him*. She gave a shaky, nervous little laugh as he tilted her face up to his. "What? Ah...no."

"But you were speaking of dolls," he teased lightly, still ignoring the man behind her.

She blushed, moving just a step back, sliding one hand up to link with his. "You caught the tail end of an unusual conversation," she said, forcing a smile as she turned her body slightly, lifting her gleaming eyes to Konar, lust all but radiating from her tense body.

Ronal lifted a brow. "Hmm. I see...I think." Then he turned his eyes to the king, and flashed him a very toothy grin, fully aware his fangs had yet to retract.

Konar quirked a smile. "A sad, disheartening conversation on my part, I fear," he murmured, touching one hand to his heart, then to his lips, his eyes on Caet's face the entire time.

Ronal pulled her more firmly against him. "'Tis a hard thing to hear something we do not want to hear," he said obliquely, resting one hand on her waist. The other hand he started to rub in circles on the other hip.

"Harder still, when you wonder if you could have done something that might have stopped it from happening." Konar's eyes were focused on Ronal's hand, a muscle jerking in his cheek.

Ronal wrapped both arms around her, nudging her with his cock, the shaky sound of her breathing reaching his ears. One hand rose to cup her breast, feeling her heart pounding heavily.

Her voice unsteady, she said, "I think I'm not hearing all of this conversation… Ronal…" One hand rose to press against his hand, as though to still it.

The other hand cupped his hip and brought him more fully against her, whimpering as she rocked her pelvis against him. Ronal turned her around in his arms, bringing the back of her body against his front as he stared at Konar, and Konar watched Caet. "He is talking about whether or not he should have done something, to keep something," Ronal murmured against her ear. "Keep *you*? Is that what he wanted?"

Sliding his hands up, he cupped her breasts, plumping them together through the shirt and smiling as Konar's eyes flashed and a rough groan escaped him.

"Keep me?" she repeated, her eyes glassy. They moved to Konar's face and she flushed as she realized he was still there, that she was indeed letting Ronal fondle her in front of an old lover.

How long... Ronal wondered, as he skimmed one hand down the front of her body, cupping her mound in his hand and grinding the pad of his palm lightly against her, listening as her breathing picked up, as her heart started to pound faster and harder, as the slick moisture from her cleft saturated her breeches.

"Aye...I wanted to keep you," Konar said gruffly, watching them through narrowed eyes. "But that is not meant to be, is it now?"

Ronal's arms loosened just slightly, and he let Caet step away when she pressed back lightly on his chest.

The Mountain King moved so swiftly, Ronal's eyes were hard-pressed to follow as he went from standing ten feet away, to right in front of them, his eyes intent on Caet's flushed face, his heart pounding inside that massive chest. "But I want something to remember, vampire. Fuck her while I watch."

Then he reached up and tore Caet's silken lace-up blouse away, his eyes rapt on her naked breasts.

Caet sputtered out, "Um, I do believe I have some say in this."

Ronal pulled her back against him and slid his hand between her thighs and rubbed her clit, lowering his head to nip her neck. Caet's breath left her in a rush and Ronal felt her acquiescence even before she said, "And I say yes..."

With a sly grin, Ronal eyed Konar over her shoulder. "Be advised, *Giani*. What I do, I do of my own free will...and because I like the idea of knowing it will linger in your mind and torment you," he said as he wound the laces of her breeches in his hand. With a sharp jerk, the lacing broke and the waistband loosened around her smoothly rounded hips. "Think of that, next time you know a lover is nearby and watching."

Konar's eyes flickered for just an instant, but it was enough. He had known that Ronal was watching from the shadow of the trees, and still he had touched her. Cool, calculating bastard.

Then Ronal shoved the elvish prick out of his head as he turned his woman around and sank to his knees, his hands at her hips, stroking downward and taking the supple leather of her breeches as he went.

She gave a shaky laugh when her trousers were stopped by the lacings of her boots. "You've already destroyed one pair of breeches. Pray do not rip apart another," Caet said when he started to simply rip them away.

Grinning up at her, he said, "'Twould be easier, milady, if you did not wear such burdensome clothing." But he untangled the cloth enough to find her boots and unlace them, tossing them aside so he could finish pulling away her breeches.

His hungry eyes traveling up the length of her, he slid his tongue across his lips, around his fangs, eyeing the pale, gleaming beauty of her ivory body standing in the fading light of the wood. "Such a lovely thing you are," he rasped as he reached out, cupping her hips and drawing her against him. Nuzzling her belly, he lifted one thigh and draped it over his shoulder, opening the folds of her sex. He pushed his tongue inside her, his fingers digging into her ass as the walls of her sex clenched around him. Bloody hell, the feel of those silky tissues convulsing around his tongue had his cock jerking as he recalled what it felt like to have his length buried inside her when she did that. The sensation was almost more than he could take.

Behind him, he heard Konar's ragged breathing. Rolling his eyes up, he stared up the length of her flat belly, over the sweet curves of her breasts so he could meet her cloudy gaze. Pulling back, he muttered, "Is Konar watching you?"

Of course, he was. But he wanted her to look at the other man. The minute her eyes met the dark gaze of the elvin warrior, her body stiffened, her eyes widened and her nostrils flared, a flood of cream flowing from her.

Erotic, isn't it? Ronal purred into her vulnerable mind. *Feeling another man's eyes on you while your lover touches you...*

She climaxed into his mouth with a scream, her knees collapsing under her. He held her weight against him as her body bucked and writhed under the lashing of his tongue.

Only when the rhythmic clenching passed from her pussy did he let her slide down to collapse into his lap.

Konar's heart would explode inside his chest, if he had to keep watching this. Matiro had warned him, time and again, that his mischievous streak would get his ass in hot water.

No, it hadn't. It had gotten his dick into a painfully hard state and no relief in sight. If he had just moved back when he sensed the vampire, he would have walked away without being in this state. Unsatisfied, still...but he wouldn't be tormented with the image of the dark-haired, green-eyed Gatekeeper laying her slim supple body on the earth, running his hands up the length of her torso, cupping those lovely pale breasts, pinching deep rose nipples as he lowered his head to catch one in his mouth.

Caet's lips parted on a shaky sigh and her head rolled limply to the side, her eyes once more meeting Konar's. His cock jerked, rather insistently this time. With a growl, he tore open the heavy buckle that secured the thick leather belt at his waist, freeing his cock and stroking it, watching with hooded eyes as her eyes roamed down his body to stare at his blood-engorged length, his hand pumping up and down with sure, steady strokes.

Ronal chuckled as he sat back on his haunches, shrugging out of his shirt, revealing a pale, muscled chest and arms, his skin nearly as pale as Caet's. Sourly, Konar thought, *They shall have children as white as ghosts, as skinny as rails...* Ronal's fingers quickly loosened the lacings that held his breeches closed over the hard ridge of his cock. The lacings fell open and his cock sprang free. "He's hungry for you, Caet," the vampire whispered as he spread her thighs apart.

Konar grunted, and fought the urge to command, beg, plead...anything to sink his aching length inside that sweet, wet little pussy. Ronal ran his thumb along the wet slit, opening her completely, the naked folds gleaming with her cream. The scent filled Konar's head and he wanted to ravage. Curling his hands into fists, he moved in, almost hypnotized by the sight of the vampire and his lover...*Konar's* lover. His lips peeled back from his teeth in a feral snarl, a growl rumbling in his throat.

Ronal pushed into the sleek, tight entrance, groaning as Caet arched up and wrapped her thighs around his hips, pulling him hilt deep within her. Holding her hips in his hands, he lifted his lashes and met Konar's eyes as the

Elf King stopped only inches away, his hand wrapped around the thickness of his cock, his eyes dazed, but feral.

Ronal flashed his fangs and snarled over Caet's naked body. "*Mine!*" he bellowed, his mental shields dropping. Pure vampire magick rolled from him, a magick that all but robbed one's will. Fear would follow, but Konar was as powerful a man as Ronal, his magick in the earth nearly as powerful as Ronal's own form of magick.

But the force of Ronal's power struck him like a fist across the temple and Konar's steps wavered, his lashes lowered. "*Fuck.*" The whisper was furious, dazed, almost like that of a man coming out of a drug-induced dreamsleep. He turned, stumbling away to the treeline of the small clearing, bracing one hand against a tree, his other hand still wrapped around his cock, now pumping back and forth furiously.

Ronal focused his gaze back on Caet. Her eyes were nearly black in her pale face, filled with both terror and hunger, one arm rising to shield her breasts, the other lying open beside her head. "Shhhh...never fear me," he crooned, lowering his mouth to lick and tug lightly on one pert, pink nipple, his hands plumping the firm, silky breasts.

Pulling out slightly, he slid back in slowly, setting a gentle rhythm until her hands came up and fisted in his hair and her breathy gasps turned into demanding, hungry cries for more. Lifting his head, he looked into her eyes and saw only hunger. With a pleased curl of his lip, he rolled onto his back, pushing her up until she sat astride him.

Her head fell back, and he felt the ends of her long silken hair caress the taut skin of his balls. The muscles in her tummy flexed as she rolled her hips, riding him slowly.

With her face lifted to the sky, her breasts outlined in the silvery light of the now risen moon, Ronal felt his heart stop in his chest. Staring at her, he realized just how close he was to the edge of a leap he hadn't wanted to take with her...but it was too late...he was already there. Staring at her as she took him in the moonlight, in the full view of an old lover, Ronal felt the last of his protective barriers dissolve as he fell completely and irrevocably in love with her.

Chapter Eight

Daklin found him two days later.

"You know, I understand that my people are a little unlike what you are used to. I realize that some of them can be quite the arrogant bastards." Conversationally, the elf continued, "I find myself hard-pressed to not want to disappear completely and totally from time to time. Or at least I did. It is not so bad now…I missed them. I needed to come home. Just like you needed solitude."

Then the elf slid him a questioning glance, one pale gold brow cocked. "But two days? Complete and total disappearance, Ronal? You will have people worrying."

"I am in love with her, Daklin," Ronal said.

Daklin's eyes closed and a sigh escaped him. "Not Caet. Please not Caet," he murmured. He shook his head. "It will not work. She is the heir—she will be *Esrine*. You cannot stay here, so far from your Gate. This will bring only heartbreak, my friend."

Ronal turned his head, revealing his hollow, flat eyes. "Aye. Only heartbreak."

He turned his gaze back to the north and sighed, the sound weary and tired.

Daklin took a breath, pressing his fingers to his brow. *Damn it.* "Have you slept? Fed?"

"No." Laughing, Ronal said, "Is there a point? You might as well take my head off now and be done with it. Save me the pain. Now I have the pleasure of living as my father did, two millennia or more, loving only one woman, a woman I can never have."

Daklin settled on the cliff next to him, more than two hundred miles from the heartland of the clan. "You came a very far way," he murmured, his eyes on the moon rising in the distance. "Did you hope to outrun it?"

"No. I thought of ending it," Ronal said. Rising, he braced his legs against the winds that rose from the chasm. "There's a stream of fire that flows from one of the caverns down there. Fire will kill me as surely as a sword through my neck."

Daklin froze, his eyes on Ronal's body. Barely daring to breathe, he started to free the hook at his waist, the long cord sliding into his hand as he rose, shifting his body to hide his actions. "Rather extreme—don't you think you should wait…"

Ronal turned glittering eyes to meet his. "Waiting will not change anything, Daklin, my friend."

Fuck. Daklin sent out a summons, calling for Cray and Arys, although he knew they wouldn't reach him in time. If he caught him—

Ronal's rusty chuckle had Daklin's eyes narrowing. "Be at ease, Daklin. If I was going to end it, I would have done it when I arrived here yesterday, and you would have been too late."

"Is that really the best answer you could come up with?" Daklin asked, his throat tight. "Love is wonderful, it sounds truly grand. Aye, and an impossible love is a burden to bear."

In a low furious whisper, he demanded, "But to end your life?"

Ronal shook his head. "No. It is the worst possible answer. Although for a time, it seemed the only feasible one." He turned away from the cliff and strode away. "I know better—truly. But it burns me, in my belly, in my heart, in my soul. More than a thousand years, and so many women I've known. And the one that holds my heart in her hands is one who will never be free."

Daklin wrapped his climbing hook and cord away, turning to Ronal with troubled eyes. "Is it truly love? You have known her mere days, a few short weeks."

Ronal's mouth twisted in a rueful smile as he lifted his face to the night sky. "I feel like I have known her my entire life," he said. He walked back to the cliff and spread his arms wide.

Daklin hissed out a furious breath as Ronal stepped into the open air. His mortal form went plummeting to the earth but before Daklin could even draw the hook back from his waist, a mist enshrouded the vampire and when it cleared, a huge, black winged hawk was flying upwards. His beak gaped open and he screeched, his green eyes staring at Daklin for a long moment.

The elf sank to the earth as the hawk flew away, his wings beating at the sky.

"I do not think I ever want to fall in love," he said into the silent night, running the *diame* cord through his fingers.

"Too much bloody trouble."

* * * * *

Cray's wings beat furiously at the sky and his eyes were tearing from the speed of his flight. *He would not. No. He wouldn't.*

A soft voice whispered to him, "Why not…you did…"

Cray gritted his teeth. Damn it all. He would not have the ghost of another person dear to him haunting him. Bad enough that he walked with one foot in the realm of men and the other in the world of power. He would not be haunted by the voices of people he failed to save. Or those he should have let go.

Cold, clean air burst into his lungs as he opened his mouth for a breath, forcing as much air in as he could before he shut his mouth, blocking off the airflow. Too much oxygen, this high up would freeze his heart. Sharp eyes caught the start of the cliffs and he folded his wings around him, dipping low. Daklin hadn't said how far they had traveled, so he would have to search for the picture he had gleaned from the elf's mind during that furious summoning.

Just then, a black hawk screeched from just above him.

I am not so far gone that I'll truly follow through with my dark thoughts.

Cray opened his wings, halting the descent and then he flew back through the air, hovering as the hawk circled around him, watching him with empty green eyes.

A sigh of relief escaped the fallen one as he recognized the vampire's winged form. "You are such a bastard, vampire," he said softly, shaking his head.

The hawk merely screeched again, as he started back toward the heart of the wood.

* * * * *

Fatigue burned through his muscles, ate at his mind as he kited through the air. The cold air rifled his feathers, his nares as Ronal flew higher and higher. He was over the heartland of the wood now, circling thousands of feet above the ground, and somewhere below him, Caetria waited.

He had caused her pain with his sudden disappearance. In his heart, he could feel the echo of her pain, like a phantom shadow. Ronal kept his thoughts hidden deep within, unwilling to let them slip out, in case she was picking up any stray thoughts or feelings from him. Bad enough he was a fool in love with a woman he'd never have. Mustn't go leaking his thoughts all over her.

A shadow flew between him and the sun. If he could have sighed, he would have. *I am here, am I not?* he thought sourly, refusing to look at Cray and see the sympathy in his eyes.

"Aye, you're here. And you've been circling around like a vulture waiting for its prey to die," Cray said morbidly. "Or like a coward afraid to come down and face reality."

Ronal ignored him. He started to soar on a thermal, aware he needed to return to the ground, and to his mortal form. He needed to feed. He just...*what?* Ronal headed west, the sharp hawk's eyes seeing something he wouldn't have seen had he been in his mortal form.

Miles out, hundreds possibly...but dust kicking up, a line of darkness. An army. And a taste on his tongue was familiar—dark, black magick. *Cray, we have trouble.*

Cray's eyes narrowed as he stared into the distance, but he wasn't able to see as clearly as the vampire's hawk form. Just a dark blur. However, his senses were just as acute. He cursed furiously. "Time is up," he whispered.

Ronal had already folded his wings around his body, hurtling toward the earth at breakneck speed.

Cray followed suit, his eyes half closed as he concentrated.

Ronal's wings spread wide only moments before he would have hit the earth, shattering bones. The air struck his wings, acting like a brake and then a mist enshrouded Ronal's form, while he was still hovering twenty feet in the air. As Cray touched down, his wings beating the air around him, Ronal was falling to the earth, landing with his knees flexed.

Birds of all kinds came flocking around them as Ronal shook his long, lean body. Cray spread his wings before snapping them closed as he circled around the small clearing, studying the birds around them.

Waves of weariness and hunger pounded at him, so strong it felt like an outside force. Shoving it aside, he waited for Cray to speak.

"Thank you, my friends," Cray said to the feathered creatures that had answered his silent summons. Even an owl, a gray-feathered snow owl had risen from slumber. He called to her, holding his left forearm up for her to land on, and to a flock of starlings that had alit in the trees. Then an eagle flew to the ground, of all places, and waited for his orders. Eyes for the day and the night, both innocuous and deadly.

Ronal waited, his body vibrating, arms crossed over his chest as he stared at the other Gatekeeper. No words were passed, but a low hum in the back of Ronal's head assured him Cray was indeed speaking to the birds that had flocked to greet their landing.

"*Go,*" Cray whispered, launching the owl into the air. Then he knelt and let the eagle hop onto his left forearm, the claws digging into the padded leather he kept strapped there. Launching the eagle into the air, he watched as it came abreast with the owl and the starlings, flying west.

"The eagle will reach them first and let us know what we face — perhaps we are mistaken and it's a Gypsy caravan," Cray said as they fell into step, striding through the wood, leaping over fallen branches and taking old, rarely used trails, cutting through the thick untraveled growth as they needed.

"Blast it, you know damned good and well 'tis no caravan, Gypsy or otherwise." Ronal slid Cray a narrow look. "How odd, you being the positive one."

Cray smirked. "Well, we cannot both be caught in a mire of self-pity, now can we?"

"Fuck you," Ronal said blandly. A ripe scent caught his nose, and a fist of hunger struck his gut, a wave of weakness following. "Pardon me a moment."

Cray was standing just behind him moments later as Ronal tore his mouth away from the stag, forcing himself not to drain the creature. "I do not think the Elf King will mind if you take a buck here or there — the wood is laden with game."

Ronal lowered the beast to the earth and rose. "I've not killed a creature in a feeding since my second century," he said dismissively. "I need not drain a creature to feed my hunger."

"You are more than hungry now," Cray said shrewdly, his dark gray eyes narrowing on Ronal's face, studying the wildly glowing eyes, the gauntness of his cheeks. "You have not fed fully since you left your lands. Finish it."

But Ronal was already jogging down a path he had seen, one that would lead them quickly into the clan's heart.

* * * * *

He gave the orders. Even though Cray had said, "Within a few hours, my eagle will be able to let me see more clearly what we saw from the skies. Then we can plan."

But Matiro would not wait. In a calm, stately voice, he summoned his scribe to hand and gave the order. "'Tis time, my friends. We journey now to the lands of the Gate and set up a war camp there, until we know better what comes," the *Esri* said, staring straight ahead as the elves within hearing distance froze, gasps falling from their lips, eyes going wide. "Children, the elders and a small band of healers will be escorted to the Mountain Realm by an armed escort of my choosing—"

"They may use my escort," a deep, growl of a voice said only moments before the *Giani* dropped down out of a tree, lifting a brow as one of Matiro's guards lifted a wicked knife in his direction.

"Konar, so nice of you to drop in," Matiro said without batting a lash. "Very well. Those not meant for battle will not be placed in danger. At this time, I call no one to fight unless they choose. All others may join Konar and his escort back to the Mountain Realm."

"Oh, I did not say I was going."

Matiro turned his face inquisitively to the High King of the People of the Mountains, lifting one blond brow.

Konar grinned. "My escort, they are welcome to. But I will be traveling with the People of the Wood to the land of the Gate. If war comes, I will be there, for I will not rest unless I know I have done all in my power to stop it from breeching my lands." His amber eyes glowed hot for a moment and his voice dropped. "Troubled times are coming. Not just the battles...so much trouble ahead. There will be unrest for the People of the Wood. I am here to help, what little I can."

A shiver raced down Caet's spine at Konar's words. They had fought battles before, defended their lands. Why did she feel his words meant more than that?

But the cold chill faded, replaced by a hot wave of need that washed over her body as she felt Ronal appear at her back.

She had known he had returned. Had felt it, the moment he touched foot back down in the heartland. That was how it had felt, as though he had simply dropped down out of the sky.

Just like she had felt it when he sped away from the clan, just two days ago, after taking her so completely. He had carried her to her *sekrine*, and lay down behind her, holding her tightly. She woke to feel his leaving, not from her...he had slipped away without her even realizing. She had felt it as he slid farther and farther away, but the moment he left the clan land, it had been like a fist closing around her heart.

"'Tis been a bit of time since I saw you," she said levelly, keeping her voice down as her father spoke in low tones with Konar.

His sigh caressed her neck, left bare by the knot she had wrapped her hair in that morning. His fingers traced the line of her neck, making her quiver. "I saw your face every time I closed my eyes," he murmured. The muscles in her legs went limp—she leaned back against him, feeling his hands settle at her hips, his chin resting on her brow.

"Your body feels cool," she said quietly, stroking her fingers down his hand, her eyes narrowing. "Too cool. You always feel so hot to me." Craning her neck, she stared up at him, concern flooding her as she studied a face gone gaunt, eyes dark and shadowed. "Are you ill?" Caet touched his cheek, hissing as his flesh felt nearly icy at her touch. Something was gnawing at her belly, hunger, strong, insistent, a hunger stronger than any she had ever known. Damn it, maybe she was catching something, too.

With a gentle smile, Ronal caught her hand. "Fatigue." Pressing a kiss to her palm, he nodded to the conferring kings. "They are ready for this. 'Tis a good thing. The People of the Wood cannot prepare for what comes. They will need all the guidance they can find."

"Stop trying to distract me," she said, pressing a hand to his neck. And in her belly, in her mind, the gnawing, burning pang of hunger grew. Ignoring it, she focused on him, the leanness of his pale face, how brightly his eyes glittered. "Something is *wrong* with you, I feel it."

Ronal's glittering eyes narrowed as he cocked a brow at her. The high sweep of his brows already gave his face a devilish look that was only intensified by the probing stare. Caet imagined facing down the Dark One would not be much more difficult than resisting the urge to submit before Ronal's penetrating eyes. "I am fine, milady, I assure you," he said.

"Then you'll have no qualms allowing a healer to speak with you." She turned, opening her mouth to summon one, only to have him jerk her back against him. His touch made her skin burn, like her nerve endings were on fire. And still...the need inside her body grew, and now, she couldn't really focus. A healer, for him, and then for her.

"That is not necessary, Caet," he growled against her ear. "They will only tell you what I have told you. Fatigue."

"Fatigue does not make one look as though he is starving...*starving*..." Her words faded away as she finally realized what was wrong. Not just with him, but with her, she could feel the echoes of his hunger and it was driving her mad.

"When did you feed last?" she demanded, shrugging away and whirling around to glare at him with her hands fisted on her hips.

"This morn, just before we journeyed back to the heart of the clan." His eyes roamed restlessly over the gathered elves, never landing on one person long.

Hunger burned in her belly, relentless, driving, *so easy...just call one of them to you...* Caet scrunched her eyes closed, focusing, drawing air in through her nose, blowing it out through her mouth. The feeling faded as soon as Ronal's face left her vision and Caet shivered.

It truly was coming from him, the relentless sudden hunger, the whispering in her mind. "You fed, but it wasn't enough," she whispered, shoring up what mental shields she could. When she opened her eyes and stared him, the driving hunger had faded and she could think.

Somehow she was picking up on what he was feeling. *Not enough*, something murmured inside her. Not his voice really, more of an instinctive urge. *Not enough, so long...so hungry.* "You've been going without fully feeding for a while now, haven't you?"

Ronal only stared at her.

"How can you be strong enough to help us battle what comes if you are letting yourself fall ill?" she asked quietly.

"Talking to a mountain, for all the good 'twill do you," a deep, musical voice murmured.

Arys and his mate stood just beyond Ronal, and when the vampire turned and met the satyr's eyes, Caet felt something odd pass between them, a relief blooming in Arys' eyes, followed by the heat of anger. "Starving yourself, you've been," the satyr hissed, stalking to Ronal and slamming his hand against the vampire's shoulder.

Ronal fell back a step, his eyes narrowing on Arys' face. "I am not starving. I am fine—go away," he bit off.

"Unicorn's ass you are fine," Arys snarled. "Fine...that you cannot be. Not if you stumble just from that."

Caet felt eyes on them as they started to draw attention. But the anger flowing from the satyr, and the warning glint in Ronal's eyes kept her from saying a damned thing. A startled gasp left her lips as Arys lifted a lean wrist and raked it with a wickedly sharp black nail, dark maroon blood welling from the gouge.

Ronal's eyes arrowed in on the blood that was starting to drip. Arys held his wrist out and said in a flat voice, "Feed, you stubborn son of bitch. Lose plenty of blood, I can and never feel any weaker. I'll be fine come morn, so long as I am in the arms of the forest. Now feed."

Caet never even saw Ronal move, just heard a hungry desperate growl and he was feeding, his jaws opened wide as his mouth fastened around the bleeding wound. Arys' eyes closed and she heard a rough sigh escape him, saw him flinch slightly. Pepper wrapped an arm around his waist, snuggling against him, her eyes on Ronal's face, the mismatched orbs full of concern. "He is as stubborn as you are, Arys," Pepper said, speaking slowly in Mitaro, an odd accent lilting her words.

Caet watched as color returned, slowly, to Ronal's cheeks. Long moments passed, and the fourth Guardian came out of the shadows, up behind Ronal, resting one hand on his shoulder. "Enough, my friend," Cray whispered. Then he moved around, reaching for Arys as the satyr groaned hungrily, his large eyes dark and glassy with the aftereffects of vampire magick.

The satyr stumbled against his wife, burying his hand in her hair, arching her neck up as he took her mouth ravenously. But then he wobbled on his feet, a foolish laugh falling from his lips as he fell back against Cray, who steadied him easily. "Drunk, I am…drunk, pretty mine… I see two of you, oh, if only…"

Pepper arched her brows. Cray smiled. "'Tis normal, pretty witch, a vampire usually has sex when he feeds, except neither of them feels the draw of another man's body. So instead of fulfilled lust, the magick is flooding your satyr's mind and making him drunk with it," he said. With a hand under the satyr's arm, he started guiding him down the path, towards their private dwelling. "I imagine you'll be enjoying…the benefits."

A red flush bloomed on Pepper's face and she averted her eyes from the elves who had gathered to watch, moving to Arys' side. As they moved away, Caet focused on Ronal's face, the distant feeling she still sensed from him, that urgent need now filled, satisfaction in its place.

But his eyes on her ignited the other hungers and she felt heat blooming in her belly, spreading upward. Swallowing, she asked carefully, "Mayhap you shouldn't delay your feedings so much?"

He didn't act as if he heard her. Reaching up, he cupped her face in his hand, rubbing his thumb over her lip. *Come with me*, he purred inside her mind. She hesitated not one second, taking his hand and leading him into the dense trees as quick as her feet could carry her.

"Enough," he growled against her ear, whirling her around and backing her against a tree. Caet's body jerked as he ripped her breeches away and she had barely time to take a deep breath before he was between her thighs, pushing upward and into her, his hands cupping her ass.

In the shadow of the wood, unbeknownst to them, the Mountain King watched for a long second. Then he lifted his hand and laid it on the trees, whispering quietly to the sleeping earth. *A woman needs her privacy...the High King need not know...* As a shield fell into place around them, Konar disappeared into the trees.

Caet screamed as Ronal drove completely inside her, the head of his cock stroking deep, so deep it felt as though he were rubbing her heart with each thrust. His hands gripped the cheeks of her ass, spreading her wide to the cool kiss of air and she whimpered, her eyes drifting closed.

"Look at me!"

Through a thick fog of need, she heard his voice and she forced her lids to lift, staring at him through a fringe of lashes as he slowed down the rampant thrust of his hips. Rolling his hips into the cradle of hers, he rested his forehead against hers, the heat of his body burned through the layers of the clothing he still wore. "I think of you all the time. I want nothing more than to lose myself in you," he murmured, staring into her eyes.

Caet reached up, fisting her hands in his hair, her heart swelling as his words rolled through her. He canted her hips up, taking her at a deeper angle. "I think…I'd like that," she groaned, licking his lips, catching the lower one in her mouth and biting it lightly.

Against her breasts, she felt him moan just before he slanted his mouth across hers. Caet opened, taking his taste in greedily, arching her back, shuddering with delight. His cock swelled within her, and she sobbed against his lips as he seemed to grow larger.

Every deep thrust of his cock into her pussy had flames licking through her veins, had her breath catching in her chest until her lungs ached with the need to scream.

As he bit lightly on her ear, the vise around her throat loosened, her head falling back as the trapped scream worked its way free, his name echoing through the air.

Ronal licked a hot trail down her neck, his teeth raking the surface lightly. With her hand fisted in his hair, she held him against her neck and whimpered, "Please."

The hot, stinging pain was there, and then gone as his teeth pierced her neck, lingering but a moment before he pulled away, but it was long enough for that hot, wonderful magick of his to fill her, erupting inside her belly as she started to come.

Ronal stroked the tiny pinprick holes left by his bite, groaning as the sweet taste of her flooded his senses, racing down his spine, his balls drawing tight against his body.

Too many layers of clothing separated them, but he couldn't take pulling away long enough to strip them off. Ronal settled on working her shirt higher and higher, until he finally had her naked breasts crushed against his chest. His own shirt, he pulled away for a second and tore it open, sinking back against her and groaning with pleasure.

Lifting his head, he stared at her face, the softly glowing purple of her eyes misty. A smile curved her lips as she shuddered in his arms, her entire body going into racking shudders. Each convulsion made her sheath tighten around his dick, a slow, thorough caress from tip to shaft as he fucked her.

He buried his face against her neck as he pulled out, the slick, hot walls of her pussy clenching and squeezing around him, drawing him closer and closer. He pulled almost completely out, taunting himself before driving his sex back inside the hot, honeyed well of her pussy, again and again until he bellowed her name against her neck and came, his seed erupting from him in hot, vicious spasms that arched his back with each explosion.

"Hmmm," he murmured long moments later, gently tugging her away from the tree and turning so that his back was braced against the smooth bark of the willow-pine. "I think I can think clearly enough now... Can we slip back to the discussion without being noticed?"

The sound of her giggling was like music to his ears.

Chapter Nine

They weren't unnoticed, but she hadn't really expected that to happen. At least she was clean—they'd stopped by the bathing pools to wash up and change.

Caet smoothed her hair back as she waited for her father to approach her. *I will not blush.* She reminded herself of that with every step that brought her father, the Elf King, closer to her. The Lady Asmine walked close behind him—thinking of her as mother was too alien.

Caetria had no mother for almost as long as she could remember. But they looked like...well, they looked *together.* A mated pair, finally reunited.

As her father stopped before her, Caet lowered her head respectfully. "'Tis somber news we have received today," she mused, after he brushed his hand down her still damp hair.

"Indeed," Matiro said on a sigh, his eyes studying her face. Lowering his head, he said quietly, "Sometimes, if you put duty before your heart...everything in life seems to fade away. Do not fade away, Caetria, my beloved daughter."

Her eyes studied his face. "What are you talking about, *Da*?" she asked, frowning.

He smiled, a tired smile that did little to soften the harsh lines of his face. The *Esri* had begun to age of late, his eyes revealing more and more weariness, lines starting to fan out from the creases, deep slashes appearing in his cheeks. No longer did he look the ageless ruler he had been for centuries. Hugging her against him, he said, "In time, 'twill make more sense to you, *vaetcha*. Konar's guard will be guiding the artisans, the Elders and young families, our pix friends, all who cannot fight, they will guide to the realm of the Mountains. You may choose to join them—or travel with your cousin to his lands."

She arched a brow. "I am a warrior, *Da*. Where the battles lie, is where I must go," she told him, shaking her head.

A smile creased his face. "I knew you'd say that. That is why I was preparing to ask you to lead them to the lands, with Daklin serving as the guide," Matiro said, guiding her over to where the Gatekeepers were standing in quiet conversation. Ronal had left her with a brush of his hand down her cheek and a smile. When she moved to them, he held out his hand for her, and she automatically took it, unaware of her father's gaze on the gesture, or Daklin's.

"Where will you be, my King?" she asked softly, lifting her gaze to her father. "Should you not lead the people into these lands?"

His eyes restlessly roamed the clan's heart, their gathering place. "I have things I must do here, before I can seek safety. Shields must be erected, the ancient places of worship must be hidden from enemy eyes. And the retreat of my people is to be guarded."

Silence fell. All eyes turned to the High King of the Elves as they heard his words, softly as they were spoken. His guard stepped forward, fire in their eyes. "Ever begging for your mercy for speaking out of place," one said, falling to her knee, lowering her head. Another took up, bowing as well, as he continued, "Protecting the people is the job of the warriors. Protecting you is our job. We shall make sure their retreat is guarded, and you must go with them."

Matiro arched a brow. "No. Protecting my people is my first duty," he said levelly, dismissing the guard.

The two on bended knees exchanged glances. It was the man who said, "You must go with them, my King. Your safety—"

"Is of no consequence if the enemy can find where the people have gone," Matiro said, his voice icy, his eyes filling with frost as he turned and stared at his guard. "My decisions were made long ago. Do not dare to question my actions, or the decisions behind them. Remove yourselves from my presence until you recall who is *Esri*."

The two guards rose, faces flushed. As they slid away in silence, the High King of the People surveyed those who continued to watch with doubtful eyes. "I am one man— but I am the most powerful enchanter among you," he said quietly. "There are times when duty calls for more than just a leader's ability to lead. Right now, it is time to protect. And that is what I will do."

His eyes landed on Caet's face, lingered there for a moment and then he looked to Daklin. "I have two powerful, capable leaders before me. If I cannot follow, they will lead on," Matiro said, his eyes gleaming with knowledge, Caet thought. Something he knew that they didn't.

Caet felt a tightening in her chest as she watched him, a fear. He had a gift of foretelling, unreliable, but very powerful.

Da... But she couldn't ask him, not now.

Somebody was watching her. Lifting her eyes, she met the soft, misty gaze of her mother. There was something in her gaze that Caet just couldn't understand. As she stared into those eyes, she started to feel lost, caught in some warm, unknown place, magick she didn't recognize flooding her body, as she joined hands with another.

Blackness, foul and dark…bearing down upon them with a speed neither of them had been prepared for…

A hand touched her shoulder and Caet shuddered, smothering a shaky breath as she tore her gaze away, whirling around, her eyes burning, her head pounding, a distant roaring in her ears. Dimly, she heard her father speaking to her, but his voice seemed muffled and odd. Automatically, she fell into step behind him as he gestured to the path that led to his *sekrine*.

What had happened?

Death bearing down upon her, yet she had felt sure and certain—ready. Caet would never welcome death so easily. Licking her dry lips, she kept her eyes fixed on her father's back, between his shoulder blades as she followed him.

Ronal moved even with her, ducking his head close to whisper, "So pale. What frightened you so?"

Caet swallowed and shook her head. Softly, she whispered, "I don't know. I was looking at my mother, and I felt…as though I was someone else." The warmth of the afternoon did not seem to touch her, leaving her cold, rubbing her arms for warmth as they took the final curve to her father's private dwellings.

From the corner of her eye, she saw Ronal's face turn to the side, studying somebody behind him appraisingly. She moved on through the open door to her father's *sekrine* and moved aside, crossing the room to curl into her customary place, a heavily padded window seat that looked over the land. From his place on this little knoll, he was in the center of the clan, in the very heart of it. Just to the east, less than half a mile of trail and forest away, was Caet's *sekrine*. His guard lived in various small dwellings around the king, never leaving him without protection. As Deltan and Tavis, the head of his personal guard, moved into the *sekrine*, Caet watched them.

They would not be able to save him…

Scrunching her eyes closed, she pressed her fingers to her forehead and muttered to herself. What in the hell was wrong? Trying to shake it off, she opened her eyes and watched as the rest of the small party filed in, the Guardians, her mother, her father's scribe, and two tall warriors. Ather and Calla were the leaders of the warriors within Clan *Esriat*. Calla was also one of most powerful enchanters in the clan, nearing her first millennium, and one of Caet's first teachers in the arts of enchantment. Her eyes were on Matiro as well, dark and worried.

Ather was one of the elves ungifted with any magick, beyond what all elves shared, an earth sense that many earth witches could only aspire to attain. He was an anomaly among the Wood elves, slightly shorter than most of them, and built like an oak tree, solid and thick, with red-gold hair that would fall in waves around his face and shoulders if he didn't keep the locks shorn meticulously short.

The warrior was in his fifth century, and in all that time, one would think he would learn to hold his tongue a little better.

"My King," Ather said, striding forward with the ease of an old friend. "You must understand, my warriors seek only to guard your safety."

Matiro cocked a golden brow at Ather as he settled into the plush, navy cushion on the carved hiargas wood chair. He hooked an ankle over his knee and rested his chin on his fist as he studied Ather. "I'm aware of their intentions," the *Esri* said quietly. "However, my safety is not as important as the safety of our people, Ather. You, a warrior, a soldier, should understand that better than any other. The wellbeing of one must sometimes be risked for the good of all."

"Not the king's," Ather said firmly, folding heavily muscled arms across his wide chest.

Matiro rose from the chair with a speed that caught many by surprise. "*Especially* the king's," he bellowed. Outside, the wind in the trees died and every last animal fell silent. Lowering his voice to a grim, low growl, he repeated, "Especially the king. Because if I am not willing to risk myself, how can I expect my people to risk themselves to protect their own? The king is one of the most well-equipped warriors for the task." He came down into the small throng of people and looked from one to another, his eyes dark and stormy. "This is an end to this foolish talk. I will do what I must, as we all will. Have you forgotten the kings of ancient times? They lead people in *battle*. Is there a safe place for a king to lay his head in battle? No. As my forefathers did, so will I."

Ather stood staring at the Elf King in silence, and finally his eyes fell away. Calla moved forward, pausing by Caet to squeeze her arm gently. Reaching the king, she knelt down, the ends of her long silvery-brown hair brushing the ground. "It will be as the *Esri* wishes. My men and women seek only to care for the king we love so much. But our duty to the clans must come first," Calla murmured. She rose slowly, her eyes meeting Matiro's, and forced a smile. "Long has it been since we have even thought of serious battle. Forgive them, if you would, Matiro, old friend. They are younger and many have never known wartime."

Matiro returned to his seat before speaking, his eyes moving from Calla to Caet. Caet suspected there was something he wanted to speak of, but wouldn't, not while she was there. "Yes, it had been an age since we have had reason to fear for our safety, our way of life. But that doesn't mean we stop thinking. War is no place for softness…and make no mistake, we are at war."

Caet swallowed, her mouth going dry. He knew what was to come. Not from experience, but from something more. How much more did he know?

Matiro saw the knowledge bloom in his daughter's eyes, knowledge that he knew more than he spoke of. He also saw how she reached for Ronal's hand, watched her lace her fingers with the vampire's. There was a bond forming there.

A knot inside his chest loosened ever so slightly as he looked deeper and saw just how strong the bond had become already. A strong, steady mate…his lashes lowered, hooding his eyes. All would be well for her, in time. The vampire would stand by her.

She loves wisely, Asmine murmured into his mind, moving closer, her body coming into contact with the side of the chair. *A kind man, in his own way…and wise, powerful. He goes unafraid into the unknown, but not foolishly.*

He is like his father, Matiro said. *And that man was one of the greatest I've ever known.*

Later, as they gathered around the great table, laden with food, the officers speaking with the Guardians, planning in low voices, preparing, Matiro felt bitterness well within him.

His daughter, that precious child who had been his only happiness for so long, and he wouldn't be able to see her reach out for her own happiness. With a frown darkening his face, he sat, hands steepled before him, his eyes on the organized group of men and women in front of them.

His daughter, along with Calla and Ather, would have to lead the People of the Wood into battle.

Unless Matiro was able to deliver a blow so severe, their enemy would know not to try to force through the wood.

* * * * *

That following morning, Caet slid the rest of her belongings that must go with her into two enchanted pieces of gear, a small one at her waist, a slightly larger one that would be carried over her shoulder, designed to hang low enough that it would not interfere with the quiver she had already donned. Fighting knives of a dozen different sizes and styles were hidden on her body and *Fier*, her enchanted blade, slid into a harness straight down her spine.

Only decades and decades of training gave one the ability to wear all without worrying it would tangle. Her bow, she drew from two carved hooks over the hearth, running her finger down the string of lotus-silk. Her father had carved this bow for her, more than a hundred years earlier.

"You fear for your father," Vay murmured, her lilting voice echoing through the nearly empty room.

"Aye," Caet murmured, her eyes still on the bow.

"He is a powerful man, a wise one. Follow you, he will," Vay assured her.

"I cannot be so certain, Vay. I look into his eyes, and I see...a farewell. He is already prepared for what is coming. He knows somehow." Caet added a few more tunics to the pack after testing its capacity with a light touch. Plenty of room, although she had already tossed in carving knives, fletching knives, eating knives, a flute, a dozen pairs of sturdy leather leggings, and several pairs of boots, not to mention half of the tunics and vests she owned. She added a couple of books and a supply of colors and paper. There was a lot of waiting coming. She didn't want to be bored.

A hot shiver ran up her spine, and she started to feel the earth beneath her feet as she walked, even though she was standing still. Inside the stillness of her *sekrine*, she felt the wind moving against her face.

Ronal. A slight smile curved her lips as she reached up, brushing a stray lock of hair from her face. Catching her lip between her teeth, she glanced down, a moue forming as she studied the sturdy, simple clothing she had donned. You didn't go traveling through the wood wearing spidersilk and *diame* threaded shirts. And she knew the plain dark clothes didn't make her unattractive. So why did she suddenly want to rip it off and pull out the soft, pretty silks Vay had already packed away?

Vay giggled. "Never primp, Caet. He makes you happy you are a woman, yes?" Her sparkling silver eyes started to dance, and Caet felt the blush deepen, her face flaming with it.

"Hush your mischievous mouth, pix," Caet muttered, pressing her cool hands to her hot face. "'Tis time to go."

Licking her lips, she looked around the room and whispered, "I do not know if I am ready to leave this place."

Vay's eyes flooded with tears. "Want to go with you," she said, her wings fluttering in a gentle back and forth motion as she lowered herself to the ground. "Damn this fragile hide." She studied her small hands and the delicate muscles before she looked at Caet.

"We're not all warriors, Vay," Caet murmured, leaning over and hugging her friend. "And that's a damn good thing. I'd make awfully ugly clothing if you weren't around. And this place would be a mess."

Vay sighed, shaking her head. "Would be good, for once, a pix to be the hero," she murmured, squeezing Caet back. She moved away then, standing in the middle of three simple cases, all enchanted. Save for Caet's furniture and a few odds and ends, all of her belongings were packed away.

"Vay, the *Giani*'s guard is waiting for you," a soft voice said from the doorway.

"Bother the guard," Vay muttered, but her wings fanned the air and her slight frame rose as she waved her hand. What Caet hadn't placed in her packs was now floating on pix magick, a gentle magick that manipulated the air and wind.

"Pack away clothes, all we good for," Vay whispered, her voice tight and choked.

"Vay—"

But Vay was already moving out the door, her wings beating madly, the cases rising into the air even as the lids were lowering on them. "She doesn't want to leave you alone," Ronal said as the pix disappeared around a bend in the path, the cases floating along as though tied to her by strings.

"No. We have been together since she was but a babe. A troublesome child, always into everything, with more mischief than five of her kind combined." Caet watched the path, until even the faint glow of pix dust had faded from the air. "I shall miss her."

She sighed as Ronal's arms came up and wrapped around her, bringing her back against him. His chin rested on the crown of her head and for a long moment, he just held her, his warmth seeping through her clothing, penetrating her chilled body. "It's time to go," he finally whispered, stroking his hands up and down her arms. "Are you ready?"

With one long, lingering stare, she looked around her *sekrine*, gathering up her two packs. "I am ready," she murmured, sliding the larger pack on her shoulder, hooking a small hole over a small metal protrusion on her utility strap. One flip of her hand would release the belt, leaving her unencumbered and ready to fight.

Ronal studied the two packs with a bemused stare. "I see you understand the idea of traveling light," he said, shaking his head.

She grinned at him, patting the pack on her hip lightly. "Enchantment wards...let us pack a great deal more than you would think," she said. "Haven't you ever noticed Daklin's?"

With a roguish wink, he said, "I do not pay as much attention to him — although I have seen that he never runs out of the pretty clothing he likes, always has those little bells for his hair."

Caet laughed. "He is vain, my cousin. Always has been — I admire that about him." She fingered the lock of hair she had woven a string of tiny crystal beads through. "There is something to be said for a man who understands good grooming."

He laughed. "I have better things to do with my time, and my hands, than braid hair," he said, bending to nuzzle her neck. "Come evening, I'll show you."

Chapter Ten

Cray lifted his arm as the eagle came winging in. The force of the wind blew his hair back from his face as the huge bird of prey spread its wings, breaking its descent. The bird landed on Cray's forearm, its claws digging into the heavy leather bracer.

The fallen one whispered gently to the bird in a tongue none of the elves could place, scratching its neck and crest for a moment before lifting the bird and staring into the striated brown eyes. The bird's pupils widened and its head slumped, falling into a light sleep as Cray's magick slid into the bird's mind, filtering through the simple thoughts and seeking out the spell he had laid the day before.

As the vision unrolled before his eyes, Cray felt the eagle's presence hovering on the edge of his mind. *Shhh...'tis well, little brother,* he whispered, letting more power slip from him into the raptor's mind. The bird's faint presence became foggier as he drifted back into the embrace of sleep.

The army was now before him, the vision of it stretched oddly, all the colors more vivid, everything more intense. His own eyes started to water just from the intensity of the panoramic scene spread out before him. The raptor didn't breathe the same way either, and soon, Cray's lungs started to burn as he merged more deeply with the bird.

Skimming his eyes over the organized regiments below him, he said aloud, "Three thousand strong easy, my friends. Magick workers, smells like sorcery, but fouled. Moving at a fast pace, too. They will reach the edge of the elves' land within two days, maybe less."

It was as though hearing from a great distance as Daklin asked, "Young or old? Are we facing power or wisdom?"

Cray had to wait until the eagle soared lower. He stared through burning, streaming eyes, seeing through the vision as the land unfurled below him. "Young, mostly. Very little experience here...*fik*." A familiar scent of power came whispering to him on the wind. Gatekeepers had a peculiar kind of magick, one that allowed them to sense the Gate's energy and power. It was like no other Cray had ever come across, and all Gatekeepers had it. The older the Keeper, the more powerful the magick. This was faint, but there were many sources, coming from all directions.

"They have Gatekeepers with them, at least a half dozen," Cray said, tiredly. There was anger, but mostly, he felt sheer exhaustion. Would this never end? Gatekeepers, men and women who should have been incorruptible, yet they stank of a dark foul magick that almost hid the scent of their other powers. And the lower he flew, the more powerful the stench of their evil became. "They've been tainted."

Her voice was softer, confused, as Caet asked, "Tainted? How can the bird tell? What does that mean?"

A low murmur that Cray couldn't distinguish followed as he started to pull out. He had seen enough. But right before he broke the connection, he saw a face...*who*...

* * * * *

"I saw someone that I know, that I've met before," Cray murmured later as he walked alongside Ronal, Daklin and Arys.

"Who was it?" Daklin asked.

Cray shook his head, scowling. "I cannot remember," he growled, running a frustrated hand through his hair.

"Getting forgetful in your old age," Ronal commented sardonically.

Cray shot him a dark look. Thunder rolled through the air, wind whipping along the trail. He forced a deep breath into his lungs, trying to relax the tension that had mounted in his body. His anger was getting the better of him now. "You recall the name of everybody you've met in your years, *kenani*?" he drawled.

Arys muffled his laugh, shaking his head. "Horse's asses recall no names," the satyr murmured. Then the amusement faded from his smiling face and he asked, "This face, this man—for a reason, you saw him. In time, you will remember."

Cray blew out a breath. "I've that hope, my friend."

* * * * *

Matiro lifted his hand from the mirror that Daklin had enchanted with his Gatekeeper magick. As he did, the image of his daughter, Ronal and Daklin faded. "Tomorrow, they will be here tomorrow," he murmured to Asmine, staring at his reflection.

Asmine moved up behind him, wrapping her arms around him, snuggling her face into the hollow between his shoulder blades. "You can journey on, join our daughter. I...I can do this," she murmured, voice husky.

Spinning around, Matiro caught her up against him, one arm banded around her waist, the other cupping her face as he stared at her, studying that dear, beloved face. "No, Asmine. I'll not hear this from you as well," he said in a whisper-soft voice. "I am where I am meant to be...with *you*. I will face all that comes, simply for the chance to be at your side again."

Tears filled her eyes as she turned her face to kiss his hands, and the touch sent hot little licks of fire spearing through him. "Matiro, all I ever wanted was to return to you, and to Caetria. Now all I want is more time."

He ran his fingers through her hair, feeling the silken tresses slide through his hand like rain. "Soon, we shall have all the time we could ever hope for." A soft sob shook her body and he held her tighter, lowering his lips to her brow. "Shhh, beloved. All will be well."

"I am not afraid for me," she whispered passionately. "I have known my time was coming for decades, as I fight harder and harder not to get lost in the world of power, and it grows ever stronger, like a riptide that seeks to pull me under." She rose on her toes, putting her face next to his as she rasped, "'Tis you being with me that bothers me. The people *need* you. Caet needs you—"

"Caet will be fine," Matiro said, laying a finger across her lips. "In time. And I am weary, Asmine. Too many centuries are weighing down on me and I can feel in my bones that it is time. Do not fear for your daughter—she is no longer alone."

"You make it sound so simple," Asmine cried, as she started to pull away from him.

Slowly, he released her, watching as she started to pace. "So simple," she repeated, her hands flexing and relaxing, small bursts of light erupting from them in her frustration. "So easy to just accept that we await our deaths here. Like you think *I* can accept that you shall perish with me. That is not what I wanted."

"'Tis not our deaths that we await," he murmured, moving up to her, catching one hand that was wrapped in magick. The heat of it tore through him and he shuddered, teeth clenched, as his body absorbed it. "'Tis the lives of our people, the protection of our home, all that we hold dear. And you have not realized something."

Lifting her hand to his lips, he pressed a hot, open mouthed kiss to it, moving from one finger to another, biting each one gently, swirling his tongue around it, moving down her palm to press a kiss to the pulse that beat madly under the fragile shield of her skin. "I have loved you, all these years, waited for you to return, fighting the despair you feel inside you as though it were my own. We are a soul-mated match, *michan*. I felt your every struggle as though they were my own," he whispered, using his grip on her wrist to pull her to him. "Every failure, every success was one I shared with you. When you cried at night, for loneliness, for heartsickness, I felt and tasted every tear. Yet you think I can walk away from this thing you must do and not share it with you?"

He fisted his hand in the front of her robe and with one harsh jerk, tore the fragile lotus-silk away, leaving her long, lithe form naked. "No," he rasped, pressing his mouth to hers as he bore her to the ground. "Where you go...I go. Your battles and mine are the same, as it should always have been."

* * * * *

"How far does it go?" she asked, relishing the ache within her body. There was no inch of her that Matiro hadn't touched. Actually, she was quite certain she had gone over every last inch of his long, handsome form. A slight smile was tugging at the corners of her mouth as Matiro linked his hand with hers.

Asmine could feel the line of enchantment wards that still slumbered in the earth. It wasn't the same form of enchantment as the barriers around the clan had been—nothing active—just a slumbering magick. That was why it hadn't been destroyed in the attack.

"As far as the wood runs," he replied. "I've been laying it down for decades now. It has had some time to age, to ready itself. It will not be enough to stop them, but it will give them pause. And kill many before it burns itself out."

Some of the weary pain was gone from his face. A purpose now filled his eyes. Asmine snuggled against him, running her hand down his naked chest. For a little while, shame had filled her, knowing he had suffered even though she had left, just to keep him from that suffering. But she had awoken with her mind and heart clear, for the first time in ages.

It was as it should be. Finally, she understood that.

"What is left, we will face, together," she murmured.

"Yes," he whispered, wrapping his arms around her and she cuddled deep into his embrace, feeling his long powerful body against hers. "Together."

* * * * *

Caet felt it in her bones when the first foul evil breeched her home. With Ronal wrapped around her, his silent presence warming her as she slept, she had felt safe, protected, loved...but the sweetness of those moments shattered as their enemy brought darkness upon the Wood of Glynmare.

Her heart stopped within her chest, and her breath was trapped in her lungs for long moments as hundreds upon hundreds stole into their lands. Lives had ended because of these men, and the bitter taste of blood spilled for power was heavy in her mouth.

The very sky darkened, wind blowing with monstrous force. Slowly, she sat up, staring at the sky through the open weave of her tent, her body shivering. Cold racked her, an icy freeze so intense it made her body ache.

"What is going on?" Ronal asked, his voice alert, tense.

Daklin's voice rang out as he called the camp to attention. Horns sounded down the line, each one rousing the next camp. She tugged a tunic on before she scrambled out of the tent, her hair blowing into her eyes as she met her cousin's gaze.

"They are here," she whispered as he strode across the clearing between his tent and hers, his brows drawn low over his crystal blue eyes.

"Perhaps a storm, an attack?" he asked.

Shaking her head, Caet whispered, "No. 'Tis them. I feel their feet walking upon my land, bringing their awful magick."

* * * * *

Remero and the master stood side by side as the gale swept through the wood. The storm had started the moment they had entered the wood and was just now lessening in its fury. It had slowed them down a full day, slogging through ankle deep water and fighting a wind that seemed determined to knock them off their feet.

Branches cracked and fell from age-old trees. One tree, an ancient giant, came crashing down and killed the sorcerers who hadn't been able to move out of the way. Thirteen of their number dead, and they hadn't even begun to fight. "From where does the unnatural storm arise, Master?" Remero asked, as cold water snaked inside the bespelled leathers he had donned. They should have kept him dry, but this rain soaked everything. Pouring down, as if giants of old were dumping buckets from the sky.

"Blast it, I do not know," Master hissed, his rheumy eyes staring out into the downpour. "Setting up camp and 'tis not even time to break for a meal. We've traveled only six hours today. *Six*!"

"We will make up the time tomorrow, wake early, now that the storm seems to be passing," Remero said smoothly. "Does not feel like a natural storm, though. It feels…angry."

The master bit back the snarl that rose automatically to his lips. It did feel unnatural. "There is no magick in it," he murmured, tugging on his grizzled gray beard. "It is just a storm. But I sense life within it."

The rain drizzled to a stop as they stood there. Remero sighed in relief, ready to settle down in his bed and rest, warm and dry, a night of peace and quiet before they routed the elves. Wouldn't be an easy task, that, even with their numbers in the thousands.

But an eerie, howling wind started just as they turned to go into their tents. And it kept up, all through the night.

* * * * *

Caet wrapped her cloak around her shoulders, smiling as she imagined how unprepared the army on their tails must be. The people had been prepared for some sort of disruption. The strangers in their land hadn't known.

Ronal came hurtling to the earth and moments later Daklin swung down out of the trees to land beside him. "Storm clouds gather in the west, all wrapped around one locus," the vampire said, grinning wickedly. "As cold as it has become for us, I imagine 'tis much worse for them."

Daklin's face was grim, but a fleeting smile lit his eyes. "Aye. I even taste snow on the air. Should they tarry too long, they shall be caught in one of our winters. Unprotected," he added, watching the skies.

Cray was winging in, his small troop of feathered scouts flying around him. The birds alit in the trees, starling, owl and eagle landing side by side, all gazing at Cray with rapt eyes as he dropped to the ground, spreading his wings wide as he shook them. "'Tis cold, very cold. Ice is forming on my wings," he muttered, rubbing his hands together. "Trees have gone down and Kip tastes blood in the air. Some of their number will not reach the clan's heart."

Kip, the eagle, screeched as Cray said his name and then he tucked his head low as the fallen one started to scratch his crest.

Under the weight of many eyes, Caet fought not to squirm. "My father is ready for them, regardless of what they bring," she said calmly, even though inside she was a mass of nerves and fear and terrified grief. She badly wanted to be back at the clan's heart. Very badly. Alongside her father as he did whatever it was he felt he had to do. "He and the Lady Asmine are waiting. This foulness that enters our land shall regret bringing itself upon us."

Then she looked to Daklin and nodded. "'Tis time to move on, cousin. Your lands are still a few days away, even at the pace we keep."

* * * * *

Why he was waiting, she didn't know. Asmine could scent them on the wind, they had drawn so close. Yet Matiro had not activated the wards. He sat calmly in the tree, further out than she, one leg drawn up, his elbow resting on it. The other leg swung back and forth and he looked as casual, as relaxed as he would if they were just taking an afternoon for themselves.

His eyes were watchful, but his face was serene.

Softly, she said, "I love you."

Those golden-tipped black lashes lifted as he gazed back at her.

"I never stopped," she whispered, a smile tugging at her lips. "And there was never another after you." Even on nights when the loneliness had almost torn her to pieces, she hadn't sought the solace of another's arms. It would have been empty.

A smile lit his face and he looked younger. "I know, *michan*. But it means a great deal that you tell me so," he murmured. He rose and walked the thick tree limb like a cat, his eyes trained on her face. Kneeling in front of her, he watched her as his long-fingered hands came up to cup her face. "My beloved."

She caught her breath just as he lowered his head, slanting his mouth across hers. That sweet, rich taste of him flooded her senses and she moaned into his mouth as she opened wider, sliding her tongue out to stroke it against his.

A deep sigh moved him and he pulled back, brushing her hair away from her face. "Are you ready?" he asked, his eyes gentle on hers.

With a slight smile, she replied, "As long as you are by my side…always."

He pulled the *diame* cord from his pouch as she rose, tugging her own loose. It had been years since she had done this. But the cord settled into her hands like an old friend, and in moments, they were swooping down out of the trees, landing lightly on the earth. She took his cord from him, looping it out of the way and tucked her own tree gear away. Then she dealt with Matiro's as he knelt on the ground, drawing a blade from the sheath at his biceps.

Dark maroon blood flowed from the shallow cut he made in his palm. Salt came from a tiny vial that hung from one of the loops at his belt. Then he planted his palm on the ground, lifting his eyes to hers.

She felt the look clear down to her toes as it warmed her. "I am ready, my King," she murmured, nodding at him.

He grinned. Then his lashes lowered and his lips started to move as he woke the old wards.

She felt the magick as it rippled down the line, spreading outward from them, north and south, easily ten meters wide of magicked earth, miles and miles long. Her hair whipped back from her face—the earth groaned beneath her feet.

"Mat?" she whispered, using the name she had called him in their early days together.

But he didn't answer. He may not even have heard her as the magick burst through him, spreading out to the trees, the ancient tumbled rocks, waking the ward spells in the ruins around them.

"By the ancient ones," she murmured shakily. "How did you create this?"

The enchantment hadn't just been in the earth. It had slept in the trees, in the rocks, in everything that was connected to the earth. *That is how…it is connected to the earth, the wood. And he connected to it.*

No wonder he had insisted only he could provide this kind of protection. It would respond to none other but him. Fear rippled through the air like a river that had broken free of its dam, but when it struck her, it simply flowed around her. The stench of fire filled the air. Then smoke, so thick she couldn't see Matiro through it.

The earth rumbled again beneath her feet, causing her to spread her legs wider to stay on her feet. Huge booming noises started to fill the air, like the very earth itself was speaking to them.

Finally the air cleared and she looked across the small patch of earth that separated her from Matiro. Nothing around them had changed—so why did everything feel different? "Heavens bless me," she prayed. "What did you do?"

"Everything I could," he responded, rising. His face was flushed, eyes glinting wildly, and his voice was rough and gravelly.

The magick has drugged him, she thought, watching as his steps wobbled just a little. He chuckled, pressing one hand to his temple. "'Tis a grim thing I've done. I should not be feeling so light in my heart."

She went to his side, sliding her hand under his arm and easing him to the ground beneath a large thisa oak, pressing the tips of her fingers to his temple. His skin was hot, and she could feel the rapid beat of his pulse under her fingers. "You are drunk on the power," she murmured, smiling down at him. "It will pass. Do you want some water?"

He jerked her into his lap, grinning at her foolishly. Cupping her crotch in his hand, he started to circle his palm against her mound. Asmine shivered, her eyes widening, tongue sliding out to wet her lips. "I'd rather have this," he breathed into her mouth just before plunging his tongue deep inside.

Asmine whimpered — but before she could even wrap her arms around his neck, he had stiffened, pulling his mouth away. His head fell back, eyes wide and troubled. "I hear them...they are close."

Mind still spinning, mouth humming from his kiss, Asmine blinked and stared up at him, trying to understand. Laying her hand against his cheek, she started to simply bring his mouth back to hers. But as soon as her skin touched his, the link between them opened, and the voices and scents and sights in his mind flowed into hers.

First ward...fire. He thought of each one as hundreds on the front line touched it. Pillars of flame erupted from the ground, swallowing them whole. Sorcery flared as some tried to force the fire out with their magick, but the wild energy only fed the magick.

Soon, the cool touch of Death whispered through the ancient forest, as she came to collect her newest souls.

Chapter Eleven

In the front line, there was disturbance. Remero stood on the saddle of his horse, balancing easily as he tried to locate the source of the turmoil. It took very little…smoke and the stench of burning flesh drifted to him. Fire. The soft, quiet whisper of enchantment slid along his senses, and he swore loudly. "Son of a bitch!" he bellowed, leaping from the horse and running at an unnatural speed as he tried to reach the front of the line.

The fools would try to kill the fire with magick. It wouldn't work.

How in the hell had a ward escaped their notice?

"Stop the march!" he ordered. "Stop the march!" Under the commands the master had laid on them, many of them still marched forward, despite the resistance coming from the front of the line as they tried to resist the force of those behind them, all but crushing them to death.

"Stop the damned march!"

Finally the soldiers seemed to hear him and the marching slowed, then ceased.

What the bloody hell is going on? Master demanded from his place at the rear of the company. *What insane magick is this?*

"Enchantment," Remero growled. "Fire ward, I am thinking." He leaped onto a fallen boulder that lay in the middle of the path, the high cliffs to his right, the winding trail blocking his view until he had gained his vantage point atop the boulder. "Aye, 'tis fire."

He could see the front of the line, some three hundred feet in front of him, where they had finally slowed and then stopped their onward march.

And just beyond that...pillars of fire were slowly dwindling down. Through the flames, he could see dark shadows on the ground. Dead men and women who had breeched the ward. Some still burned, but a wall seemed to keep them from retreating once they had crossed a certain point.

Their screams echoed in the air as they died, and all around him, his army of soldier sorcerers stared wide-eyed at the destruction before them. "Bloody hell," Remero breathed. "How did they do that?"

* * * * *

It was a full hour before the fires cleared and died away completely. A full three before they had regrouped and counted the dead. Along the line, there had been fifteen flanks, two units in each flank, and each unit had roughly a hundred men, two units side by side where the terrain allowed it. Each unit marched in four regiments of twenty-five men, the leader at the front. They had invaded along every discernable path into the wood, paths left unprotected by the destruction of their shields, and now visible to mortal eyes.

A quarter of the front units had died. More than seven hundred troops, dead. More than half of that number had been because they had been pushed into the ward by their own troops as they marched blindly on under the orders of the Master. The blind fear by which the Master ruled had cost them a quarter of their men.

As Remero stalked through his encampment, his face set in a dark scowl, he swore an oath to himself. One day that old man would die. None lived forever. And when he was dead, Remero would remember this, remember what blind fear had cost them.

"How many?" the Master demanded, ducking out of his tent as though he had been waiting for Remero.

"Seven hundred, Master," he said, stopping in his tracks and dropping to one knee. The old man wasn't going to take this lightly.

A ghostly aura swirled around the Master as he battled his rage, the power swelling inside him. "Seven hundred," he rasped, his gnarled old hands clenching into fists. "Seven *hundred*?"

"Aye," he replied. "The front units lost a quarter of their numbers, many of the Captains died instantly."

The Master started to pace, his eyes swirling and glowing. "I do not believe this," he muttered, shaking his head, his staff smacking the earth with each labored step. "Why did you not see the ward?"

Remero lowered his eyes as he fought to reply, *Why didn't you?* But he rather valued his own neck. "It would appear that the ward was sleeping, waiting for the creator's touch to awaken it," he murmured.

An angry hiss escaped the Master. "Only one would have such power. Blast the king, it was his magick that did this. Rot his soul." Eyes gleaming madly, he crooned, "Oh, he shall pay for this. I shall give that bitch daughter of his to my most depraved men."

"Why, thank you, Master," Remero said, smiling widely, as he oozed charm and goodwill. They needed the old man calm, and they needed him clearheaded. Which meant grounding him again, using whatever means necessary.

The Master glanced up, startled, and then he chuckled. "Do not flatter yourself. You do not have the taste for blood that I am wanting—I want her to suffer pain and humiliation. You are more into humiliation," he said, shaking his head. The glow of rage was dying, replaced by calm, rational eyes. Or rational for the Master.

The old man was getting more and more tetched every day.

"Is the ward used up?" the Master asked, lowering himself to the padded chair set up outside his tent.

"It would appear. Have you anybody you would like to…test?" Remero said with a wolfish grin.

"Hmmm…the bitch I called to my bed last night had the nerve to hesitate when I bade her to kneel before me," the Master murmured, his eyes smiling. "Fool bitch. She will do."

Remero suppressed a sympathetic smile for the poor woman. He would hesitate as well, if ordered to go down before a creature as wizened as the Master. But she should have hidden her repulsion better. Time to die…and better her than him. "So shall it be," he murmured, rising and offering one final bow before he went to seek out the sacrificial goat.

But the shivering, sobbing woman who was thrown into the line, amongst the burnt corpses didn't erupt into fire. On hands and knees, she stared at them, a sob falling from her lips, eyes shining with both fear and relief. And then...she rose and took off running, away from the company.

"Shall I bring the wench back?" one of the Captains asked, his eyes on the pale flash of skin they could still glimpse as she tore through the wood.

"Why bother? She'll be dead by morning in this unnatural cold. If some wildling beast doesn't get her," Remero said, shrugging. "We have an unknown number of whores around. Now we have one less nonproductive mouth to feed."

She had been a pretty thing though, a mortal who didn't speak their language, with dark blonde hair, fine and straight, and soft blue eyes. Spirit still shone in those eyes, as evidenced by her fleeing. A truly broken woman would have just lain there, silent, perhaps sobbing.

Ahh, well. Perhaps he'd run away screaming as well if he had the choice of either dying or possibly sucking on the Master's withered old cock. No. He would run. No question about it.

* * * * *

She ran so swiftly the ground blurred beneath her feet. This strange, unknown world was terrifying. Tumbling through some rip in the fabric of her own world, it had taken her months to stop questioning her sanity.

She had yet to accept her fate, though. Passed from one pair of cruel hands to another, unable to speak their tongue, she had feared that her nightmare world would never end.

But when they had thrown her into the mass of still smoking bodies, she had known why. They wanted to make sure the magick fires she had seen burning the men were done.

Throwing me to the fucking wolves, she thought, dashing a tear away. Bad enough she was stuck here, away from coffee, the internet, her books, her *life*. Now they were trying to kill her. And she knew why. That old man she had been forced to serve last night. He had seen the distaste in her eyes and he was making sure she understood that none dared to defy him.

"Kiss my butt," she muttered, her lungs burning as she tumbled through the undergrowth, ignoring the branches that lashed at her legs. They could see all the damned stripes they had left on her with the beatings.

But then she crashed into a hard form, and a scream erupted from her throat. *Damn it! No!*

"Shhh…shhh," a soft voice murmured.

Arys studied the woman in his arms. She had passed out, pure terror most likely. She had run as though the hounds of hell had been at her heels. And when she'd screamed, it had been in his mate's tongue.

"Why be you here?" he asked softly as he turned around and started back. In his mind, he called out to Cray and let him know that he wasn't going to make the front of the enemy line. Not with this sad little burden.

She whimpered in her throat and he brushed a gentle kiss across her brow. "Come…let me take you to my wife. She will give you ease," he said quietly. Then he whistled and waited as the wildling 'corn, one of Faryn's get, came running down the trail on nimble, nearly silent feet. "Sorry, boy. No time for feeding and resting as I promised."

* * * * *

Cray circled overhead, sighing as Arys whispered into his mind, *I've a mortal here, unconscious, bruised, beaten, and terrified. Taking her to Daklin's Gateland, I am. I cannot leave her alone here.*

Of course he couldn't. *I'm moving in now, watching, I can do. Go on with you, satyr.*

Then he alit in the treetop, using the dense foliage for cover as he started to walk along their tops, a gust of wind elementals beneath his feet as a floor.

The scent of death was heavy in the air.

What had Matiro done?

* * * * *

He felt each of their deaths upon his heart. Some had been truly evil, even from the first. Others had been young, misguided...but their minds had been fouled by their leaders' touches.

Matiro lifted his head from Asmine's lap as they drew closer to the next ward, still unaware. But they wouldn't be caught off guard so easily this time. Already, they had split their units into smaller numbers, sending scouts ahead, two-by-two.

Not that it would matter this time. This ward was set all around them, in the trees, not in the ground.

Finally, as many had crossed into the ward's boundaries as it would hold. That was when one of the leaders bellowed out a warning.

But it was too late.

This time, they were close enough that some of the screams carried to them on the wind from miles away.

* * * * *

The following afternoon, Remero kept his place closer to the front, but not on the front line. After the losses they had suffered with the fire ward, he wasn't taking any chances. Each unit had a pair of scouts traveling ahead of them by nearly a mile.

A magickal tether kept them connected with their Captain. Should that tether be broken, then they would stop.

But so far, so good.

The Master still rode at the rear of the company, speaking in mental commands with Remero from time to time. "All is silent, Master," he murmured as it drew closer to the time for the Master to start his nagging again.

Keep your eyes open…this is unlike the elves to let us travel this far without confronting us. They may have more wards —

Remero's eyes narrowed. Just under the hooves of the horse in front of him, for the merest second, a dark gray cloud had lingered. Now it was gone. But a metallic taste flooded his mouth as premonition raced through him.

"*Pull back!*" he roared, jerking the reins of his horse, guiding the battle-trained steed back, farther away from that line. "A ward! Pull back, *now!*"

But it was too late for some. There were no screams this time. It was in eerie silence that they died, the very air around them thickening, phantom hands sliding from nowhere to crush the life from the men.

Tricksy bastard, they were facing. Because ahead…the scouts had passed the barrier, and were safely on the other side, staring back as the life was slowly choked out of the men and women.

Once no more life breathed within that line, from all around them, white forms slid into view. Ghostly apparitions, staring at the company, all up and down the line. A terrible laughter echoed from them and then they were gone, their forms fading away and drifting upward into the sky like smoke on the wind.

The ward of the unnamed dead had been activated. So many Elvin souls, lost to battles over the years, their bodies never returned to their land, but their memories never gone.

It had been a heartbreaking ward to construct, as Matiro relived conflict after conflict, war after war, calling upon the souls that had pledged allegiance to their lands, their people, and their safety. Their blood stained the wood. Matiro had used his blood to call out to them, blood to blood, bond to bond.

"They have lost a thousand men now," he murmured to Asmine. "One final ward before they reach us."

"What is this?" she asked, her eyes haunted. So much blood, so much death.

"Fear." His eyes closed. "They have until nightfall. It comes with the setting sun."

* * * * *

Caet's eyes were nearly black in her face. Ronal held her against him, rocking her. The deaths were weighing on her heart. Death by magick was brutal at times, and she was connected to the earth through her father. She had felt them all like a knife in her gut.

"So many deserved their deaths," she whispered. "But some were little more than children."

Ronal stared around her, carrying her in his arms as he strode through the wood.

Daklin's lands were closer than she had thought. He could scent the wild Gate magick in the air. "Hush, sweet," he said softly. "Block it off if you can. This is not something you must experience."

"Aye, I must." Her voice was hollow, empty. "Each death is one more that will not bring danger upon my people. I should know each one."

Ronal scowled, and held her tighter to his chest as her body started to shiver. She would *not* know each one, damn it. Daklin was fully capable of blocking the rampant emotions and fear she was feeling, once he had her on the elf's land.

He had long ago learned that he couldn't take the deaths of the guilty inside, not if he wanted to stay sane. In his lands, violent death was something he had to battle endlessly as invaders from the high north pushed ever close to his lands. For one thousand years he had watched as they fell under the might of his own armies, and he grieved for the young lives ended.

But when war was waged, lives ended. And he would rather it not be the lives of his people.

* * * * *

Daklin hunkered in the tree, watching as the last of Clan *Esriat* crossed the farthest northeastern border of his lands. Too much of the battle Matiro was waging on the invading army was leaking through to the elves, the sensitives and the blood kin to the king, who shared a bond with the earth.

Caetria would be bearing the brunt of it—and it was near to driving Daklin insane before he shut it down. She was too inexperienced and might not block it away on her own.

He sliced his palm open and laid it on the tree, whispering to the resting wards. The only sign it had been activated was a whisper of wind that blew through his hair. The moment it locked into place, a silence fell through the wood, bringing a shield between them and the rest of the wood.

He glimpsed a silvery coat in the distance, narrowing his eyes and focusing. Arys and the wildling 'corn tearing through the wood like demons. The Gate magick was what powered his enchantment. It would recognize Arys and allow him passage.

Daklin released the climbing rope at his waist and launched it through the air, swinging down to the ground, pulling the hook free with an expert flick of his wrist.

Each ward activated would reverberate through the wood and Daklin would monitor it as they set up camp and started building their own defenses. The energy of the Gate would let them build powerful wards, nearly as powerful as the wards surrounding the wood had been before the dark, evil magick had ripped through it.

And in time, the protections would be stronger.

The Gate was never unprotected, and it fed off the energy of the lives in two worlds. They would be safer here, he told himself as he jogged down a hidden path that led to the heart of his lands, where the Gate lay. *I should have had Matiro bring them here long ago*, he thought, wondering if what was happening could have been avoided.

But Matiro may not have listened. He had his own agenda, that was certain. Ducking a low-hanging branch, he followed the faded trail around the base of the cliff, the soothing sound of birdsong and forest life in his ears. Daklin fought not to give into the grief within his heart as he thought of Matiro and Asmine.

Like so many of the people, he had heard the finality in the *Esri*'s voice. The king and his bride would not walk away from this. Their lives would be given in exchange for the safety of all, something Daklin had risked many times. And he wished it was his turn again, rather than knowing his king was laying his life down in certainty, not just a risk.

The wards that lay in the earth were connected to him, and he felt it nearly an hour later as Arys crossed the borders into his lands.

Daklin lifted his head, tuning the conversation out that he had been carrying on with Ronal and Ather, his eyes going blank. Arys wasn't alone. And it wasn't Cray who he sensed.

No…this was a mortal.

A heartsick one. Daklin felt the fury of her pain and it ripped through him like the bite of a whip. *Bad imagery*…he tumbled through the morass of memories in her mind, falling into the memory that he had roused with his careless thoughts. Strapped to a post, arms chained overhead, burning, fiery pain streaking along his back and thighs…

No. It was her. Her memory, the whip cutting into her flesh, tearing it, as screams threatened to choke her. Bile rising in her throat until she choked on it, trying to turn her head so she could vomit it out but a strap had her head fastened to the pole.

Sweet mercy. Daklin tore himself from her memories with a violent wrench, and fell back against a willow-pine.

"What is it?" Ronal demanded, catching his elbow and steadying him as he straightened up.

"A refugee," Daklin muttered, his back still burning in shared memory. "Arys has her. She has been...brutalized."

"We do not need a battered soul right now," Ather murmured, pressing his fingers to his eyes.

Daklin's eyes cut to him, icy and enraged. "We do not decide when they come—a power beyond us. 'Tis not our place to question it," the Gatekeeper declared.

Ronal's sigh echoed in Daklin's ears. "'Twill not be easy," he whispered, shaking his head. "If any of the soldiers break through and make it here, she will be witnessing violence she doesn't need to see. She must be in awful shape to have shaken you so, without you even seeing her, Dak."

But before they could say more, Cray came winging in and his arrival stopped the conversation, as all present turned to him, waiting to hear what he had seen.

But Daklin couldn't stop thinking of the woman.

* * * * *

The final ward was the smallest, but it was the most powerful. Like a huge ribbon unfurled in front of the land, it would hold only so many. Less than three hundred would be inside it when the light of the moon activated it. But almost half their numbers dead, before a battle even began.

And they still had to breech Asmine's Sorcel wards.

Death by fear, not a pleasant way to go.

Their screams would echo around the heart of Matiro's kingdom, and he would hear them as they died.

Closing his eyes, he focused on the simple, soothing touch of Asmine's fingers gliding through his hair.

The echoes of their footsteps on the land rippled through his mind, like a timepiece, counting down the time.

Closer…

Closer…

His lashes lifted and he murmured, "'Tis time. Last one."

Seconds later, the screams started. Matiro rolled to his feet, and held out a hand for Asmine. She rose, lifting her face to him. "'Twill take time," she murmured. "I will have to take a short journey…"

Matiro's eyes watered as light coalesced and then exploded around Asmine. When it cleared, she was gone.

Turning his eyes back to the west, he listened as the screams echoed throughout the wood, destroying all the peace and solitude that had once been theirs.

"We shall take it back," he promised. Might take time, he thought, echoing Asmine's words. But they would have it back.

* * * * *

Asmine gathered the power, funneling it through the Gateway that linked the world of power to her world. She slid back to realm of men seamlessly, like she had never left and when her eyes opened, they glowed.

Energy crackled off her skin, her hair and robes floating around her body. Her eyes cut to the ground. "A river would be lovely...must first make its path."

Straight into the earth, she funneled the power. Her eyes could see it, a misty form, like a heat mirage, cleaving through the air, the earth, and the bedrock beneath.

The ground started to tremble.

That was when she split the power, one of air, forcing breaks and cracks into the earth, weakening it. The other shaft of power continued to funnel down through the bedrock, until it broke through to the core of the earth.

There, a river of fire bubbled and hissed. And when she tore open the escape path, it started to flow.

Through all the tunnels and breaks in the earth her magick had rent, until it had nearly reached the surface. And then she slammed down a shield, blocking it from reaching the surface.

With a gasp, she fell to the earth and forced her eyes to clear. "That should do it," she whispered, brushing her hair away from her face with a shaky hand.

To mortal eyes, all was well.

But when she looked beneath the surface, there was a river of fire, following the line of magick that Matiro had staked out years before, separating their land from the rest of the world.

Closing her eyes, she wove an illusion, hiding the river of fire under the guise of a faux shield. They'd attack it, thinking to power it down. And under the force of that, her shields would give and the river of fire would erupt from the earth.

"It will scar the earth," she whispered, turning her eyes to Matiro.

"The earth will recover. In time." He settled behind her, curling his body around her. His chin came to rest on her hair and she settled into the warmth of his body. "Do not be afraid."

A tremulous smile curved her lips. Honestly, she said, "I am trying not to be."

* * * * *

The shaking of the earth was felt in the Gateland, all the way to the Mountain Realm, and far to the west.

Remero said, "We should pull back. Already we have lost nearly half our men."

The Master rasped, "No! I have not come this far, lost more than a thousand sorcerers that I bred and trained as my warriors just to turn back in the face of enchantment and paltry earth magick. All this is, blast it. The satyr's doing, I know it."

"Master Damis, I know you wish to see them all die, that you need this land to take control of the Gate. But we are at a disadvantage now, weakened. Let us retreat, for a few months, a year, regroup," Remero said.

An unseen hand closed around his throat, blocking his air. Gagging and gasping for breath, Remero fell to his knees as Damis approached him. "*No*...they thought to throw me out, to take the Gate from me...it was *mine*!" he bellowed. "And look what happened!" He held up wrinkled, gnarled hands, widening his rheumy eyes. "I spent all my life in a fine, strong form, taking care of that blasted Gate and then they think to tell me I am not to use its power for my own ends. It was *mine*. They aged me...they damn near killed me...then they let that satyr take it, bloody perverted wretch of a creature."

The hands around Remero's throat opened and he sucked in a painful breath of air as he fell to his belly. "My apologies, Master," he gasped, rubbing his throat, letting the chilled earth cool his hot face.

But Damis didn't hear him. "They will pay... I'll have all the Gates, and they will pay," he muttered, pacing.

Chapter Twelve

Cray jerked awake two hours before sunrise.

It had been at a council summit. A younger version of the man he had seen within the enemy army.

Nearly five hundred years ago, that had been the first time. The mortal sorcerer was being called to task for not protecting his Gate as he should. They had not found him guilty of any crime, but had he been found guilty, Cray and Ronal would have been two of his judges.

Twice more, he was called before the council, and each time, Cray saw his face, but only briefly.

And again, four hundred years later, a secret Council meeting. He had been siphoning energy off of his Gate, in the way only a Gatekeeper could. The sorcerer had spent too much time in the world of power. Some theorized that it had warped his mind.

Cray wasn't so sure if the man hadn't been warped long before. Decisions were made. He would be taken from the Gate, sent away, exiled to the Gateless land in the far south, where the snow and ice never melted. There he would age quickly, no longer sustained by the Gate's power.

But before they could remove him from his Gateland, Damis had died, going through the wood with a young man who had traveled to learn sorcery under his hand.

The man had claimed lightning, dark and black, struck down out of the air, hitting an ancient forest giant, and the oak had fallen in flames to the ground, catching Damis under its bulk. Not just one man he had seen before, but two...the student now led the army, directing the flanks with the ease of one who was accustomed to it.

And the other man—Damis, not dead these past decades. But alive, and amassing an army.

He tore out of the quickly constructed lodge he was supposed to share with Ronal. Of course, Ronal was busy fucking the daylights out of the lithe and lovely leader of the elves, the *Esria* Caet.

"Satyr!" he bellowed, striding into the middle of the clearing where they had started to build their small encampment. "Vampire! Elf! Get your asses out here, *now*!"

Daklin arrived within seconds, his eyes tired, cloudy, a bemused look on his face. "Whatever are you roaring about, bastard?" he muttered, rubbing a hand against his eyes.

Arys came out of his lodge, and Daklin slid his nude form a look. "Having fun, are you now?" the elf asked as the scent of sex and woman filled the air, heavy on the satyr's tawny skin.

"Having fun, I was," Arys muttered irritably. But his eyes met Cray's just as Ronal came into the clearing, his fingers busily securing the cords at his groin, closing his hastily donned breeches.

Caet came in behind him, a shirt skimming her thighs, hands rubbing her arms for warmth, her eyes dark and flat. Daklin scowled and directed Cray a dark look. *They get a hot, sweet woman in bed with them at night...and I get woken from my rest by a surly winged bastard. How fair is that?* the elf asked silently.

"Arys, where were you, the days when it was reported Damis died?" Cray demanded, striding to the satyr.

Arys frowned, one sleekly muscled shoulder lifting in a shrug. His brow puckered, his eyes going blank as he thought back. "In my wood, trying to court Lorne, I was," he finally answered. "Felt the massive oak crash, I did." He cocked a brow. "Had I but known how my life would change."

"A body…was one ever recovered?"

Ronal responded, "No. 'Twas burned in the fire. He was trapped under the tree and the fire burned so hot, the land around it was scorched just from the heat."

Daklin moved closer to Cray, his hair gone silver in the moonlight, his eyes in shadow. "Cray, what is going on?"

"'Twas Damis I saw in the enemy camp. And the student he petitioned the Council to take on," Cray said quietly, falling into Mitaro as elves gathered around, straining to hear him speak. "The old bastard is not dead and has been planning this for decades, maybe longer."

"Damis…"

That was Pepper. She had slipped up on them without Cray realizing it, her bi-colored eyes wide and confused. "But Damis was a Gatekeeper."

Arys shook his head. "Cannot be, Cray. Whoever it is, I do not know, but Damis…it cannot be him," he murmured, his large eyes hard, cold and angry. "From my wood, he was. Lived there centuries. Born, I was, knowing him. It *cannot* be him."

"Why?" Ronal asked quietly.

Arys didn't answer. But they all knew. He had broken bread and spent time with a man capable of that kind of evil. His wood had accepted him, given him free reign all that time, even before Arys' birth, even before he took over guardianship of the wood. "Certain, you are?" he asked roughly, one hand plowing through his sable hair. His hand lingered, brushing the curved spiral of one horn, as he waited.

"Aye," Cray said, spreading his wings wide, fanning them in agitation. His feet left the ground unwittingly and he snapped his wings tight and close to his body, landing again, grunting as a rock dug into one large, bare foot. "There is no doubt within me. 'Twas Damis. And with them is the man he took as student, the one who reported Damis' death."

"Remero," Daklin whispered, recalling the charming bastard who had visited Asquiro with Damis for a handful of years before the Gatekeeper's sudden death.

Ronal's eyes glinted with pinwheels of a thousand shades of green, his fangs bulging behind his lips as rage built. "Betrayed, by our own brother," he muttered.

Cray knew he was recalling the mortal who had served as one of the Pillar Gatekeepers, alongside the vampire for centuries on end. "Aye," the fallen one replied bitterly. "And the blasted sorcerer knows how to use a Gate's power for ill already. If he gets here…"

"He will not," Caet said quietly, stepping into the tightly knit circle of Guardians. Looking from one to another, her eyes finally settled on Cray and he felt the punch of the power that resided within her. "Not this time, at least. My father's wards have given him doubt, made him question his strength. And there is still the magick of my mother they must face. We all felt her touch upon the earth, felt it shiver under her power. Perhaps we shall even be lucky, and he will die under the force of her attack."

Then she moved forward, standing eye to eye with Daklin, a hard, cold smile edging up the corners of her mouth. "But even if he does not, even if some survive her sorcery and travel onward here to the Gatelands, we are not without our own defenses. We are warriors, all of us and we will not fall under the hand of that corrupt bastard," she murmured, holding out her hand.

"Aye," Daklin agreed, linking hands with her, then jerking her against him for a quick hug. "Well said, cousin. We are warriors, all of us."

* * * * *

Remero rode near the front of the line as they traveled deeper within the wood.

It had taken the lives of two sorcerers to make it work, but he had worked a seeking spell, and no enchantment wards were left, not after the one they had triggered last night. It had been a nasty piece of work, something he hadn't expected from the elves, one that caught the men within it and killed them with fear, using visions of nightmare creatures and the sorcerers' own weakness to destroy them. Some had driven knives into their own chests to end the terror, while the rest of the army stared in mesmerized terror.

No, nothing left. They would reach the heart of the king's clan and find the man who had cost them nearly half their army, and he would die slowly. And the daughter...Remero had plans for her. And may her father's spirit rot in the world between as he watched helplessly.

Fall back, Remero. We need to regroup, replan our attack, Damis ordered into his mind.

Fucking old goat. Remero had suggested that very thing only this morning. But the querulous fool had refused, insisting they continue on their path, and immediately.

But he tugged on the reins of his mount and guided him to the side, turning the warsteed around and heading to the back of the company where Damis rode in relative safety, and in supreme luxury, the small, lushly appointed carriage gliding on the rough terrain with magick-hastened speed.

Are you going to release some of the hold you wield so tightly over these men? he asked in mocking curiosity, shielding his thoughts from the Master. While Remero knew he was more intelligent, more cunning than the Master, he wasn't more powerful and he didn't want to risk angering the man who had been training him for decades. *Let them use their judgment instead of blindly pushing them on?*

But the Master wouldn't. He enjoyed ruling with fear as his greatest weapon. Remero knew that well.

He was drawing even with the carriage when he felt it, an echo, perhaps, of the earth tremors that had rocked the wood the night before. His eyes cut to the head of the line as another tremor rocked the ground. This one more powerful, more intense…some people falling to their knees.

And it was as if a veil had been jerked away from his eyes as he stared into the east, where he could almost taste the power of the elves.

A river of fire, waiting just beneath their feet…and the ground weakened.

Damis felt the punch of sorcery at the same time Remero did. They should have felt this before now…sorcery wasn't a quiet magick. How had they hidden it…where had the sorcerers come from?

"They called their sorcerers back," Remero said flatly. "And we just walked right into the trap they laid for us."

Damis' reply was drowned out by the rumbling that erupted beneath them. And far ahead of them, at the front of the line nearly a mile away, the earth started to rip apart, as though fabric in the hands of a very angry giant. "Pull out, Remero," Damis whispered, his rheumy eyes drooping closed. "Get us out of here, now."

Remero had already jerked open the door of the carriage and before Master Damis had even finished speaking, he had lifted the old man out, tossing him behind on his warsteed as he whispered in an archaic tongue, his hand glowing red as he laid it on the neck of the warsteed, bespelling the steed for swifter travel. Calling out the order for retreat, he drove his heels into the steed's unprotected sides.

"Live to fight another day, Master," he said quietly.

* * * * *

Asmine shivered in Matiro's arms, her body a taut hungry curve against his.

The magick had been loosed. She had been huddling against him in fear, nearly incoherent as they waited for the river of fire to break through the earth. But then his hands had touched her, sliding inside her tunic. Shutting her mind to what was coming, she lit up in his arms, reveling in the long, heated press of his body against hers.

As the ground rumbled below them…one final time…she sighed into his mouth, "I love you, Mat."

His murmured reply, "*Michan*, my beloved…I adore you, worship you, love you with all I am," was the last thing she heard before the river of fire exploded, and they were lost.

* * * * *

Caet stumbled, the strength going out of her body.

It was as though a light had been put out — no — two of them, bright burning lights within her heart. As she fell to her knees, a sob ripped from her throat.

"*Da…Mierna*," she cried, knowing her parents were beyond hearing her.

Ronal's arms came around her and she wrapped her hands around his forearm, sobbing. "They are gone…" she managed to gasp out.

Silence fell through the wood as she cried, her body shaking in Ronal's arms.

* * * * *

Daklin felt the echo of their passing within his heart and his mouth spasmed, his throat jerking as he fought to hold back the tears. Not now. Caetria would need some time…he was here, he would make sure she got it.

Lifting his gaze, he studied Ather and Calla for a brief moment, before turning his gaze to Arys and Pepper,

Pepper kneeling over the still form of the woman Arys had brought within Daklin's lands.

"The *Esri* has gone to greet the Ancient One," he said formally, pushing the words past the knot in his throat.

Somewhere in the distance, an elf lifted a flute and played a melody, a lonesome, heartbreaking sound that was soon joined by voice after voice.

* * * * *

Caet stood numbly by, listening with half an ear, as Daklin ordered two small bands of warriors into the wood. "Check for any survivor of the enemy army," her cousin was saying.

All eyes moved to her and she nodded in silence from her position by the window.

Da…Mierna.

"They were together in the end, as they always should have been," Ronal whispered from behind, one hand coming up to rest warmly on her shoulder. She laid her hand over it, her head lowering.

"Aye. I know."

"No longer plagued by sorcery, by anything," he added gently, moving up behind her and curving one arm about her waist, sliding the other down to wrap around her, encasing her in the strong, powerful warmth of his body. "Nothing can ever cause them pain again…save seeing you, lost and alone. The pain will pass, in time."

She swallowed, hot tears trickling down her cheeks. "Aye," she repeated numbly. "And I have all the time in the world, do I not?"

Five days later, she awoke in his arms, her throat raw from another crying jag that she had indulged in, once she was in the privacy of her hastily built *sekrine*, as his hand stroked her hair, his lips brushing against her cheek. He would leave soon.

None of the scouts had found any survivors.

Three days earlier, Cray's starlings had flown in and he had wandered among them, touching one's crest, the other's breast, making odd little chirping noises before falling into silence. When his eyes opened, he brought the starling that had landed on his arm to his face and he pressed a kiss to its beak, chuckling as the bird chirped and sang. When he turned his dark eyes to them, a slight smile lit his face. "They have retreated...and their numbers are terribly devastated, less than a third of what they were."

The danger, for the most part, was over.

And Caet had a clan to regroup, lives to rebuild. None of the elves had died, thanks to her father and mother. They had never even had to wage a battle. But their homes were gone, lost in the fireflood that had been unleashed. Steam still lingered in the air and it would be months before they could even draw near, months before all the small fires caused by the fireflood died out.

And they could no longer live peacefully within the wood.

As long as the man called Damis lived, war threatened Mythe. Her way of life, gone.

The elves would go into battle now. And she would have to prepare for that. For war.

Alone.

No, perhaps not alone. Daklin would always be there, guiding her. Hell, he would make a better king to these people than she would a queen. He would not leave her alone now.

And Ather and Calla, even Konar would be there.

But Ronal would not. Ever more often, his eyes strayed to the north. His Gate was calling him, his people needed him.

As her people would need her. Damn it.

Staring down at in the dim light that filtered through the window, she studied that proud, powerful face, the harsh set of his cheekbones softened in sleep, the high diagonal slant of his brows. The sensual curve of his lips, the thick black hair that spread under him like a cape, as soft as spring rain in her hands.

Heat flooded her belly as her heart wept. Lowering her head, she pressed a soft, openmouthed kiss to his chest, moving down the hard line of his torso, rimming his navel with her tongue as she pushed the blanket aside, straddling one long, muscled thigh.

The thick head of his cock nudged her chin as she slid down and she lifted slightly, opened her mouth and licked it, feeling it jerk beneath her touch. Wrapping her hand around the base of his sex, she took him in her mouth, moving her head slowly, up and down, relishing the taste of him, the scent, the feel…as she committed it all to memory.

His ragged groan caressed her ears as she slid further down, taking as much of his length inside her mouth as she could before pulling back up. With her hand, she massaged the heavy sac of his balls then pulled away slightly, ducking her head and pressing a kiss to the furred sac, lightly raking him with her teeth.

A hoarse shout ripped from him and she flinched slightly as his hand tangled in her hair, guiding her mouth back to his cock. With a slow, subtle rhythm, she worked him, feeling the pulse of the large vein that ran along the underside of his shaft. With each upward stroke, she sucked on him, releasing the suction as she slid back down.

His hips started to rock as he rose to meet her, nudging the back of her throat with his cock, stealing her breath away. "Caet, sweet...ahhh...that feels so damned good," he grunted.

She smiled around his length and started to pump her hand, eliciting another ragged groan from him. His cock jerked, throbbed within her mouth. She tasted the salty fluid that started to seep from the narrow slit in the head of his cock. Humming in her throat, she moved faster, greedy for every rough moan, every ragged curse.

Ronal bellowed out her name and gripped her head, holding her still; he pumped the steely hard length of his cock back and forth between her lips as he erupted, his come spurting from him. She swallowed it down greedily, using her hand to pump every last drop from him before she released his still rigid sex and sat up, staring down at him.

She gasped as he rose off the pallet and pinned her beneath him, his moves lightning-quick, his mouth coming down on hers, his fingers threading through her hair.

One knee pushed between her thighs and she spread them willingly, arching her hips up as he drove inside her.

Tears streamed from beneath her lashes and silently she whispered, *I love you*.

The thick length swelled, throbbed within her pussy, the slick wet sounds of their loving echoing through the *sekrine*. His head lifted, his mouth leaving hers as she gasped for air.

Pushing to his knees, he rose over her, and she could feel his eyes on her, as sure and certain as the grip of his hands around her hips as he moved her back and forth on his length. In the heart of her, deep within her pussy, she felt his cock jerk and throb before he slowly withdrew, his eyes on her face.

He pumped again, deep inside, pulled out slowly, never taking his eyes from her face as he fucked her, loved her, late into the night.

"Caet," he rasped, his head falling back, the moonlight shining down on the carved muscles of his body, highlighting his chest, and shoulders. Shadows fell across his throat, a stripe of shadow falling across his belly, his hands.

The sight of him was so perfect, it almost hurt. He lifted her up, holding her body against him, using his hands to move her up and down on his engorged cock. "Please, please, please," she sobbed.

"Shhh," he muttered, his hot hands cupping the cheeks of her ass as he lifted, then dropped…lifted, then dropped, penetrating her so deeply it almost hurt.

The walls of her pussy clenched around him and he throbbed. Sliding one hand between them, he touched lightly on her clit and Caet exploded, screaming his name as she came with long, shuddering spasms that hugged and milked his cock, his hands working her up and down.

His teeth sank into her neck, and the hot touch of his magick rolled through her, prolonging the orgasm. The fingers of his other hand bit into her ass, and against her chest she felt a moan reverberate through him. Hot waves of his seed spilled upward inside her and she moaned out his name, rocking against him.

His arms came around her, cuddling her against him. "Caet," he whispered.

She snuggled into his chest, squeezing her eyes shut against the burn of tears.

Chapter Thirteen

Ronal was gone in the morning.

She felt it as surely as she had her parents passing. He had stayed longer than Arys and Cray had, longer than he probably should have. Weariness was heavy on him, the weariness she saw on Daklin when he was too long gone from the wood.

She rolled onto the heavily padded silk pallet, bringing the blankets to her chin, breathing in his scent.

Caet had fallen in love with him…the worst possible thing she could have done. She wasn't free to be with him. And he couldn't abandon his Gate. Even if he did love her enough to try, such an act would drive him mad or kill him.

Sighing, she shoved the blanket down and rolled to her feet. Caet had a duty to her people, as did Ronal.

She needed a bath…but she couldn't wash away the signs and scents of his touch, not yet.

Maybe later. After she had answered the call of duty, and tried to sit and act wise, and not like her heart was breaking.

Duty…

The word whispered through her mind as she brushed away a tear.

Then a memory of her father. *Sometimes, if you put duty before your heart…everything in life seems to fade away. Do not fade away, Caetria…*

Closing her eyes, she fought against the wave of pain that rocked her. Yes, nothing in life seemed truly important now. Not without him.

Do not fade away…

The words echoed in her mind as she sat before Daklin, settled into the carved *thisa* oak chair that had been given to her just days earlier. By rote, she listened and responded, one small portion of her mind focused on what her cousin was saying.

The rest of her was remembering Ronal.

"Caet."

With a slow blink of her eyes, she pulled herself back into the present, away from memories. Apologetically, she smiled at Daklin, just now noticing he had cleared her home of all others. "I am sorry, cousin," she murmured. "My mind was…elsewhere."

"Do you love him?" Daklin asked quietly.

Tears burned her eyes and she looked away, reaching up to rub her temple. Her fingers touched the queen's coronet she had received only a few days earlier. The elves didn't hold with the mortal tradition of an elegant coronation ceremony. Daklin had placed the coronet on her head after she had recited the vows most sacred to the people before a small audience.

Thus, she was queen. High Queen of the People of the Wood.

And she was miserable.

The heavier, more ornate coronet had replaced the simple *diame* one she had worn for years. It was still simple, and still small, lovely in its simplicity. But the weight of it seemed enormous.

It felt like a shackle on her ankle, instead of a lovely piece of elvish artistry, unrivaled in all the world.

Daklin's sigh was closer and she squeezed her eyes closed as his hand lifted hers and folded around her chilled fingers. "Do you love him?" he asked, his voice a little more insistent.

"Yes." Hot tears rained down her cheeks and she turned to look at Daklin, staring at him, pain ripping through her. "How can I love someone I just met? I've known him only weeks."

His smile was sympathetic, his shrug deprecating. "I've never really loved with my all heart before, cousin. But when it's meant to be—maybe it can happen like that. Maybe it is supposed to." He dropped down to sit at her feet, as she had sat so often before her father, and he studied her closely. "What do you do now, Caet?"

Do not fade away, Caetria. "I do not know," she whispered. The pain was bitter in her heart. Slowly, she whispered, "I've never wanted the responsibility of being *Esrine*. Never. But I had accepted it. Until Ronal. Now I feel so terribly trapped."

"Trapped is not a good way for the High Queen of the People to feel. All turn to you in times of trouble, Caet. The People of the Mountains, even our distant cousins by the Sea of Anyar seek out your counsel," Daklin said, his voice flat. "You cannot be the leader you must be if your heart isn't in it."

Do not fade away, Caetria...duty...heart... She clenched her eyes tightly shut, lifting her face to the sky as a cool wind started to blow, a light rain misting down upon them. "I have a duty to my people. I am my father's daughter," she whispered roughly.

"He would have walked away from it all, if he had known Asmine would welcome him."

Her wide eyes cut to Daklin. "He was *Esri*."

"He was a man, a father first. He would have risked all to be with your mother, to have his family together and whole," Daklin said. He smiled gently. "We are a long-lived race, pet. Very long...and we love deeply. Think you are the first to have discovered her mate was one who could not dwell forever in our lands? It will shatter you inside, not being with him. And truly, as you said, your heart has never been that of a queen. A leader, always...but not the queen."

"Go to your lover, Caet." A new voice joined them and Caet shivered as she watched the *Giani* shimmer into view. Damned spirit walkers, appearing wherever they choose, walking between the worlds. Konar settled himself on a padded window seat and repeated himself, "Go to him. The land will choose a ruler from among your blood kin."

Her brow creased and she shook her head. "I cannot just leave. I am—"

"One woman of the line of *Diartemes*," Konar said. "His line is plentiful, and proud, powerful. Another ruler can be found. Our people do not believe in sacrificing all for duty. For honor, yes, for pride, yes. But not for duty. If in your heart you are not happy, then you cannot give the people your best."

"*Biesten*," Daklin whispered, his eyes glowing as he turned his face from Konar to stare at her.

The word rang a chord within her. *Biesten*... freedom.

A pounding settled within her heart, magick flooding her. A bright light flooded the *sekrine*, and she squinted against it, staring at her hands, at the shadows falling across them. She lifted her head, but couldn't see where the light was coming from.

Before she could even speak, though, the sensation of a weight being lifted filled her. Her coronet had been pulled off, by unseen hands drifting out into the space between her, Daklin and Konar. It spun in a circle, slowly at first, then faster, the light that poured from it becoming brighter and brighter. And then it stopped, and an image was left standing there, a tall, reed slender elvish man, dressed in clothes so antique, she couldn't imagine how old he must be.

Konar dropped to one knee, a soft whisper coming from him. "*Diartemes*," he whispered, lifting one arm and crossing it over his chest, his head lowered.

The Elf Kings bowed to no one. Caet's jaw dropped as she stared at Konar, but then the name he had called the man connected, and a gasp fell from her as she, too, dropped to her knees.

Diartemes, the first *Esri*, who had led the elves into this part of the world, away from the lands fouled by the final battle with the *Etiocs*, the long-dead race of hideous twisted man-like creatures that fought with blood-tainted magick, and had once destroyed everything they came across.

Until they came across the elves. The people had stopped them, and eventually defeated them, wiping them from the face of the land of Mythe, long before humankind had even learned how to speak.

Her forefather. Eyes stung with tears and she lowered her face, ashamed. All he had fought for so that their people could start anew in a land they would care for and watch over, and she didn't want it, couldn't take pride nor pleasure in it.

Not all are meant to rule.

She flinched as the voice boomed through the *sekrine*. Lifting her eyes, she stared at *Diartemes* as he approached her, a kindly smile on his ageless, softly glowing face. *"Daughter mine, your heart is heavy and it grieves us all,"* he said, his voice echoing, as though he spoke from very far away. *"You must listen to your heart...that is the first duty for the People of the Wood, listening, and heeding the heart. If I had listened to reason and talk of duty...we would have stayed in the fouled lands, and died long ago."*

Tears spilled down her face, questions forming in her mind, but unable to be spoken. Her throat was too tight, too tense, and too much awe filled her as she stared at him. *Diartemes* laughed and he whispered, *"Go...follow your heart. The man who is the king has been here for ages, ready to lead."*

Daklin's eyes glazed over as she watched, and his body jerked. Slowly, he shook his head and whispered, "I cannot. I am Guardian, first and foremost. Until I breathe my last."

"A man who is bound to the land already, to every living creature in it. Your heart is here, your soul is here, your duty *is here. You've always known, in your heart, that you were meant to lead the people. So do it,"* Diartemes said. Then a burst of light exploded, wind whirling through the *sekrine*, knocking them back.

Eyes burning and watering, she rubbed at them, pushing back to her knees as she gasped for air. Through tearing eyes, she looked around.

"By the blood of the Ancient One," she whispered, her voice trembling.

The coronet was still there…but it had been reformed, reshaped. Pure *diame*, the hardest substance known, once solidified into its destined shape, was unchangeable. Adding in silver or gold would make it flexible, malleable, which was how they made their *diame* threads, their climbing ropes, and baubles.

But the coronet of the commanding Royal was solid *diame*, molded while still in liquid state, right from the mines.

Yet her coronet had been reshaped into masculine lines and angles, instead of fluid feminine curves. Instead of the deep purple moonstone that had been centered in it, there was a gleaming pale blue diamond. And it was lowering itself onto Daklin's head.

And in her palm, somehow, she held the purple moonstone, now set in a heavy filigree of *diame*.

Slowly, a smile curved her lips.

Chapter Fourteen

She rode a 'corn mount. The dappled 'corn had sauntered into the wood that morning as she prepared to leave, stuffing her belongings haphazardly into her enchantment packs.

The stallion tossed his head and stamped his foot, staring at her with commanding eyes.

"What do you want, you blasted unicorn?" she asked, trying to go around as he kept blocking her path. "You can speak to whomever you choose, I know it. So if you want something, then *say* it."

He merely tossed his head again. But now she saw the intent in his eyes. With a wild laugh, Caet leaped atop the 'corn, and they were tearing through the wood at speed unlike anything she had ever known.

Now two days had passed, and she was in the cold lands of the north, at the very edge of the vampires' lands. Her thick oiled cloak of *kekri* hide was tucked tightly around her, against the cold winds and the rain that fell erratically. Eagerness flooded her, tension and hunger and need.

He was close. Not just a few towns away, she thought as she sped through one, following an urging in her gut.

But *close*.

Once she hit open ground, away from the curious eyes of the human and breed vamps, she leaned over and whispered in the 'corn's ear, "Slow down a bit…he is near."

She didn't know if the damned thing would listen. The unicorn seemed to have an agenda of his own, urging her out of bed hardly moments after she had lain down, or so it seemed.

But he did slow. Stopped, actually, so suddenly she was nearly thrown. Leaping from his back, she turned around, staring at the mountainous terrain. Already, the small town she had ridden through was lost to sight among the twists and turns of the mountain paths.

"Ronal!"

Her voice echoed all around her. And then silence.

Nobody seemed to be there, save for the dark shadow of a hawk circling above her. Her shoulders slumped and she dropped to her knees. "Ronal." Damn it, she could *feel* him, like a warm presence that hovered all around her.

So why didn't he come to her?

* * * * *

The pale golden banner of her hair streamed out behind her as she tore through the tiny little town of *de Ankrah*, the smallest of his liege lands. The scent of her skin carried to him on the wind as he soared in the air above, his heart clenching at the sight of her.

What are you doing here, Queen of the Elves? he asked silently. The title was to remind him—she could not be his. His life was tied to his Gate, to the lifeblood of his people.

"Ronal!" she bellowed, spinning around on the ground hundreds of feet below him. Then, more softly, she sighed his name as she slumped and dropped to the ground, her entire body trembling.

Folding his wings around his body, Ronal plummeted to the earth. He shifted back into mortal form just as her head lifted, and he watched as her eyes widened in amazement at the change.

"Far from your home, *Esrine*," he said formally, studying her face. Something was different.

She launched herself at him and he stumbled back as he caught her, unable to keep himself from burying his face in the silk of her hair, his hands roaming over her back as she burrowed against him. "Ronal," she whispered. A shudder racked her body and then she lifted her face, one hand sliding behind his neck, bringing his head lower.

He groaned as she thrust her tongue into his mouth, then sharp little teeth nipped his lip. Starving for her, even though barely separated two days, he angled her head up, seeking out the sweet, rich taste that was Caet. Her body tensed and she jumped in his arms, startling a laugh as she went from standing on the earth to straddling his hips, ankles hooked just above his butt. Finally, though, he pulled his mouth away, staring down at her. "What are you doing here, Caet?" he asked gently.

"You left," she whispered, running her fingers through his hair. He leaned into her touch, watched as she tangled her fingers through the long lengths while her other hand stroked his neck.

"My Gate called me," he said wearily, leaning his forehead against hers. "And the longer I stayed at your side, the harder it would have been to leave."

Hard? It had damn near ripped his heart out.

"Would you have stayed? If you could?" she asked, her lashes drooping low to hide her eyes.

"By the Blood, yes," he groaned, crushing her to him. "I would give all I had, just to be with you always. Damned witchy little minx, I fell in love with you within moments, it seemed, of meeting you."

When a laugh bubbled out of her, he lifted his head, narrowing his eyes at her. "Not exactly the answer I had hoped for," he said sardonically. Then he lowered his head and pressed a gentle kiss to lips. "Please…please, just go. If I think too hard, I shall be unable to let you go."

With a winsome smile, she watched him from under her lashes. "You do not have to," she whispered. "I love you, Ronal de Amshe. And I have no intentions of leaving your side, not ever."

That was when it dawned on him, what was different. No simple, yet elegant coronet adorned her brow, for the first time since he had met her. "What is this?" he asked, keeping his voice neutral, even though his heart was slamming within his chest.

"I abdicated… I think," she replied. "The line of the Royals runs strong in Clan *Esriat*. The one who should lead them is now doing it. And I am free…"

"You walked away from your lands," he repeated hollowly.

"Gladly."

Carefully, he disentangled her legs and set her down, reaching up to gently remove her hands. "Return to your kingdom, *Esrine*. This is no light thing you have done, not something you can take back in a few years, or a few decades, when your heart starts to yearn for the wood," he murmured.

Her eyes watched him, puzzled. Then she laughed. "I can return whenever I choose...for a time," she said, moving back against him and hugging him tightly. "But that is not home for me. Home is with you, beside you. *That* is where I belong, not ruling a land alone, with my heart empty."

For a long moment, he did nothing. Then he cupped her face in his hands, gently, tenderly. "Be certain..."

"I am," she replied, laughter in her voice.

The laughter turned into a gasp as he took her to the ground. Desperately, he lowered his head to her neck, kissing the smooth pale skin roughly, his hands jerking and tearing at her clothes until her shirt fell open, baring her breasts. He shredded her trousers, tossing the remnants of cloth away, before he lowered his head, bringing her smooth mound to his lips, catching the hard little nub of her clit in his teeth and sucking on her.

The nubby cloth of her knee-high black boots, a few shreds of the leather trousers still tucked inside, rubbed against his hands as he caught her legs, pushing them high.

Moving lower, he stiffened his tongue and started to thrust it inside her, his body shuddering as she moved against him, rising to meet his mouth, a long, rough moan falling from her lips. He savored every sound, every small movement, as he drank from her pussy. Shifting, he moved back to her clit, lifting his hand and pumping two fingers slowly in...slowly out...measuring every ripple of movement.

As she started to come, he pushed up, jerking open the lacings of his trousers, the cold air biting his flesh before he lowered himself atop her, the sweet burning heat of her length warming him. With one long, slow thrust, he buried his cock inside her wet sheath, murmuring her name against her ear as he started to fuck her.

Slowly at first. Then faster, as her nails bit into his neck and her pussy clutched at his cock. Her hand came to his head, urging him down as she arched her neck in simple invitation. Ronal took it, unable to resist, piercing the tender flesh. Ecstasy rocked him as her taste hit his belly, her essence filled his soul, filling in all the empty hollows he had lived with for so long. *Mine...*he thought to her, delighted as she whispered aloud, "You're mine, too."

Now he understood, finally, the nickname Arys so often whispered to Pepper... *mine...pretty mine...* The knowledge that she was *his*, that he was keeping her was a heady one, and he lost all control, driving into her with near violence, lifting his mouth from her neck to bellow out her name as she screamed his, her snug sex milking his rigid cock.

As she drained him, he slowly came down to rest on her shuddering body, grimacing as the gripping contractions worked over his cock. Over and over, until she had drained him, and finally, her climax ended.

"So you wish to stay here...in the land of the cursed vampires, with me?" he asked gently.

"Hmmm...nothing I'd like better," she purred.

Eyes stinging, he wrapped her in his arms as he rolled to his back, pillowing her body with his, tucking her cape close around her nude form. "Mine," he sighed, satisfaction settling through his body.

She yawned delicately, then whispered back, "You're mine, too."

Enjoy this excerpt from
Coming in Last
© *Copyright Shiloh Walker 2004*

"So what's eating you?"

Sliding Mick a glance, Jamie lifted his shoulders in a disinterested shrug and said, "Not much." Flipping through the file on his desk, he skimmed the account information they had received, and cursed mildly the sense of family obligation that had him agreeing to drive two hours south and stay there, for heaven only knows how long.

Of course, it wasn't like he had anything more interesting to do at the time.

"You know, you've had that same damn look on your face for about the past six months, like nothing on this earth can hold your attention for longer than five minutes."

Flashing Mick a grin, Jamie said, "Well, anything having to do with your ugly mug is gonna bore me senseless in five seconds. What's your point?"

"Just wondering when you're gonna snap out of this, that's all." Mick shrugged, lifting his shoulders as he sipped from his coffee before flipping a page and studying the next. "You know, this is really a waste of time. Time and money—his money, our time."

"His money. He can afford us. And this was slick, slick and pat. There may well be more missing than what is showing," Jamie mused, eyeing the accounts.

"There is that," Mick said with a nod. "So when are you gonna snap out of it?"

"Snap out of what?"

"This funk."

Jamie sighed. "Mick, I'm bored. Okay? Just bored." He laughed, recalling the scene with Erin from the previous weekend. "I can think about business while I'm getting a blowjob, and a damn good one. Tell me what in the hell the problem is here?"

"You need to let me have the woman while you get your head examined?" Mick offered blandly.

Jamie rose, the tailored suit falling into place over his gun as he strode over to the window and stood staring out into the clear summer day. "Something is just...missing, Mick. I'm bored with all of this. Everything. All of it. Not the business, but my life. Erin was just the exact same as every other woman I'd gone out with before her. And the next one will be just like her."

* * * * *

There was something about a woman surrounded by kids, Jamie mused. Some guys tended to be put off by the sight, but Jamie loved it—loved watching women as they held and rocked, soothed and played with children.

Her laugh floated above the higher-pitched laughter of the kids as she unlocked the pudgy little arms from her leg and lifted the baby. Settling him on her hip, she answered one question after another as she wove her way through the maze of toys and games already spilled out on the floor.

The high-pitched peals of laughter and the squeak of excited voices had his head pounding again. Wincing, Jamie pressed his hand gingerly to his throbbing temple, wishing for a bit of peace and quiet. Hell, he had planned on coming down here with a feigned injury, not a real one.

Right before he could open his mouth, she stopped mid-stride and turned her head, meeting his eyes across the room. Light reflected off her glasses, keeping him from seeing her eyes. She turned her head and the chunky teenager took the baby from her.

"Hello."

Squinting against the bright light, cursing the throbbing in his head, he managed to growl out, "Hi."

"Looks like you bumped your head," she said. Without asking, she laid one hand on his arm and guided him around the perimeter of the room, sidestepping toys and toddlers with ease. "The clinic is right over here."

Moments later, laying flat on his back, eyes closed against the harsh glare of light, Jamie mumbled around the thermometer, "Is all this really necessary?"

"Company policy," she replied as she wrapped a blood pressure cuff around his arm. Competent, quick hands checked his vitals while Jamie lay there waiting for the Motrin he'd taken to kick in. Strong, cool, slender fingers wrapped around his wrist. It was just the pain that caused his pulse to race, Jamie told himself.

A subtle scent wafted over to taunt him. God, she smelled good.

Through the fringe of his lashes, he watched as she rose from kneeling on the floor and smoothed down the plain, simple white utilitarian scrubs she wore. As she turned away, his eyes locked on the long red braid that hung between her shoulder blades. Her hips swayed as she moved around the small office, gathering up paperwork, asking questions that he replied to as quickly and tersely as possible.

A soft wail rose from the other room and he waited for her to respond. When the wail continued for more than ten seconds, he asked, "Aren't you going to check on whoever that is crying?"

"It's Amy, our newborn. And she's hungry. Abby's got to get her bottle ready." She glanced at the simple band of braided leather on her wrist.

"Quite a lot of A's."

With a grin, she said, "This is the A-team. We have Andi, which is me, Abby, Alex, Amy, Aaron, Aspen, and Arnie, the pet hamster." Another glance at her watch, and a few seconds later, the tiny cry was silent as laughter and excited voices filled the air.

Her skin was smooth and pale, not a single freckle marring her milky complexion. And up this close, he doubted that shade of red came out of a bottle. Her eyebrows were the same shade and so was the super fine hair he could see scattered across her arms. Her eyelashes looked to be darker, but behind the glasses, he really couldn't tell.

"Hectic job," he said.

With a roll of her eyes, she said, "Any job that involves anybody under the age of thirteen is hectic."

"What happens after thirteen? Does it become less hectic?"

"No. After thirteen, it just becomes more traumatic. Ever had to deal with a thirteen-year-old girl who was convinced the world was going to stop turning on its axis because the boy from math didn't call the way he said he would?"

"Actually, yes. I have two sisters."

"Then you should already know what happens after thirteen."

Lowering herself to the rolling stool, she asked, "Dizzy?"

Some twenty minutes later, he was ushered out into the relative quiet of the hall, and he had to admit, he agreed with Johnson.

She didn't fit the image of a corporate thief at all.

And she smelled better than he ever would have imagined.

Her mouth, hmm, well, her mouth was probably going to be giving him some sweaty dreams for a night or two. Those naked, pouty lips put only one thing in a man's mind. And the thought had his cock stiffening up like a pike. Just the thought of her putting that mouth on him—

"Enough, McAdams," he muttered, stalking down the hall, absently rubbing his temple. "The girl is a damned embezzler."

About the author:

Shiloh was born in Kentucky and has been reading avidly since she was six. At twelve, she discovered how much fun it was to write when she took a book that didn't end the way she had wanted it to and rewrote the ending. She's been writing ever since.

Shiloh now lives in southern Indiana with her husband and two children. Between her job, her two adorable and demanding children, and equally adorable and demanding husband, she crams writing in between studying and reading and sleeps when time allows.

Shiloh welcomes mail from readers. You can write to her c/o Ellora's Cave Publishing at 1056 Home Avenue, Akron OH 44310-3502.

Why an electronic book?

We live in the Information Age—an exciting time in the history of human civilization in which technology rules supreme and continues to progress in leaps and bounds every minute of every hour of every day. For a multitude of reasons, more and more avid literary fans are opting to purchase e-books instead of paperbacks. The question to those not yet initiated to the world of electronic reading is simply: *why?*

1. *Price.* An electronic title at Ellora's Cave Publishing and Cerridwen Press runs anywhere from 40-75% less than the cover price of the <u>exact same title</u> in paperback format. Why? Cold mathematics. It is less expensive to publish an e-book than it is to publish a paperback, so the savings are passed along to the consumer.

2. *Space.* Running out of room to house your paperback books? That is one worry you will never have with electronic novels. For a low one-time cost, you can purchase a handheld computer designed specifically for e-reading purposes. Many e-readers are larger than the average handheld, giving you plenty of screen room. Better yet, hundreds of titles can be stored within your new library—a single microchip. (Please note that Ellora's Cave and Cerridwen Press does not endorse any specific brands. You can check our website at www.ellorascave.com or

www.cerridwenpress.com for customer recommendations we make available to new consumers.)

3. *Mobility.* Because your new library now consists of only a microchip, your entire cache of books can be taken with you wherever you go.

4. *Personal preferences are accounted for.* Are the words you are currently reading too small? Too large? Too...**ANNOYING**? Paperback books cannot be modified according to personal preferences, but e-books can.

5. *Instant gratification.* Is it the middle of the night and all the bookstores are closed? Are you tired of waiting days—sometimes weeks—for online and offline bookstores to ship the novels you bought? Ellora's Cave Publishing sells instantaneous downloads 24 hours a day, 7 days a week, 365 days a year. Our e-book delivery system is 100% automated, meaning your order is filled as soon as you pay for it.

Those are a few of the top reasons why electronic novels are displacing paperbacks for many an avid reader. As always, Ellora's Cave and Cerridwen Press welcomes your questions and comments. We invite you to email us at service@ellorascave.com, service@cerridwenpress.com or write to us directly at: 1056 Home Ave. Akron OH 44310-3502.

Make each day more *EXCITING* With our

Ellora's Cavemen

Calendar

www.EllorasCave.com

THE
☥ ELLORA'S CAVE ☥
LIBRARY

Stay up to date with Ellora's Cave Titles in
Print with our Quarterly Catalog.

TO RECIEVE A CATALOG,
SEND AN EMAIL WITH YOUR NAME
AND MAILING ADDRESS TO:

CATALOG@ELLORASCAVE.COM

OR SEND A LETTER OR POSTCARD
WITH YOUR MAILING ADDRESS TO:

CATALOG REQUEST
C/O ELLORA'S CAVE PUBLISHING, INC.
1056 HOME AVENUE
AKRON, OHIO 44310-3502

Discover for yourself why readers can't get enough of the multiple award-winning publisher Ellora's Cave. Whether you prefer e-books or paperbacks, be sure to visit EC on the web at www.ellorascave.com for an erotic reading experience that will leave you breathless.

www.ellorascave.com